Please Talk to Me

Please Talk to Me: Selected Stories

LILIANA HEKER

EDITED AND WITH AN INTRODUCTION
BY ALBERTO MANGUEL

TRANSLATED BY ALBERTO MANGUEL
AND MIRANDA FRANCE

YALE UNIVERSITY PRESS ■ NEW HAVEN & LONDON

A MARGELLOS
WORLD REPUBLIC OF LETTERS BOOK

The Margellos World Republic of Letters is dedicated to making literary works from around the globe available in English through translation. It brings to the English-speaking world the work of leading poets, novelists, essayists, philosophers, and play-wrights from Europe, Latin America, Africa, Asia, and the Middle East to stimulate international discourse and creative exchange.

Yale University Press books may be purchased in quantity for educational, business, or promotional use. For information, please e-mail sales.press@yale.edu (US office) or sales@yaleup.co.uk (UK office).

Set in Electra type by Newgen North America, Austin, Texas.
Printed in the United States of America.

Library of Congress Control Number: 2014957517

ISBN 978-0-300-19804-1

A catalogue record for this book is available from the British Library.

This paper meets the requirements of ANSI/NISO Z39.48–1992 (Permanence of Paper).

10 9 8 7 6 5 4 3 2 1

For Ernesto Imas

CONTENTS

The Stories of Liliana Heker

In 1966, the twenty-three-year-old Argentinian writer Liliana
Heker won the prestigious Casa de las Américas prize with a collection of short stories, *Los que vieron la zarza* (Those who saw
the burning bush). The book was published in Buenos Aires, in
July of that same year, by Jorge Alvarez, an editor whose keen eye
had led him to discover such future luminaries as Manuel Puig
and Rodolfo Walsh. A few days earlier, in June, the weak demo-
cratic government of President Arturo Illia had been overturned
by a military coup led by General Juan Carlos Onganía. Onganía
was an antiliberal ultraconservative who quickly dismantled the
workers' unions and tried to place the universities under his own
authority. The attack on professors and students, effected less than
a month after the coup, came to be known as the "Night of the
Long Sticks" because of the brutality of the assault. Paradoxically,
this repression sparked a vigorous opposition to the government
which would, years later, force the military leaders to call for dem-
ocratic elections.

At the time, Liliana Heker, besides writing short stories, was
working as subeditor of *El Escarabajo de Oro* (The gold-bug), a
celebrated literary magazine she had founded in 1961 with the

writer Abelardo Castillo. Clearly left-wing but interested, above all, in publishing good literature, the magazine continued to appear until 1974, and throughout Onganía's dictatorship, it maintained the same ideological and literary position it had before the coup. *El Escarabajo de Oro* became the centre of vigorous debates, explicitly opposing censorship and acts of violence, defending the Cuban Revolution and Third World movements and offering a platform to some of the most distinguished contemporary writers.

Later, during the bloodiest era of Argentinian history, Heker's position of resisting in situ and taking active part in the public debate did not change. In 1976, as a result of another coup, General Jorge Rafael Videla became the new head of government, and under his authority tens of thousands of men, women and children were arrested, tortured and killed or forced into exile. Hundreds of babies born to so-called terrorist women in military prisons were taken away and sold or given to families close to the regime. To justify his actions, Videla explained that "a terrorist is not only someone who carries a bomb or a gun, but also someone who spreads ideas contrary to Western and Christian civilisation."

To write under a dictatorship is, unfortunately, an all too common experience in the history of our literatures. Those who oppose a tyrant are all too often either imprisoned, killed or exiled, even though the authorities never realize that such measures, however drastic, never quite succeed in silencing a writer. The words of Ovid in exile, Boethius in prison, and Isaac Babel murdered continue to resonate for us, their readers, today. As Heker wrote at the time: 'Censorship is never infallible . . . It is the advances made by a writer against the limits imposed on him, and not a fatalistic acceptance of those limits, that change the cultural history of a country, and therefore history itself.'

Heker, true to this conviction, and faced with the option of exile, chose to stay in Buenos Aires. The strategies of survival under these circumstances are complex and mysterious, and owe much to chance; they have to be reinvented day after day. In a few cases, they turn out to be successful, and both the writer and the work manage to outlive the oppression. 'My fiction writing,' she later explained, 'didn't change at all during the military dictatorship. A novel, a short story, are always elaborate constructions and they are meant to last; in the small space of freedom that your own room conquers, you can work on a piece with a bare heart and give in to the most scandalous or audacious ideas. I will give a personal example: during the first years of the last military dictatorship, in the midst of its horror, fear and threats of death, I kept on working on a short novel about an alcoholic man and his wife that I had started sometime before the coup. This passionate and meticulous writing, this diving into my characters' intimate nightmares, rescued me, during my working hours, from the external nightmare, and it allowed me to be carried away, through the adventure of creation, from the constraining world.'

To follow her policy of what she called 'cultural resistance,' besides leading underground writers' workshops and signing petitions in favour of the Mothers of Plaza de Mayo, towards the end of 1977, at the height of the military dictatorship, and again with Abelardo Castillo, Heker founded a new literary magazine, *El Ornitorrinco* (The platypus), whose motto was taken from Oscar Wilde: 'One should always be a little improbable.' The magazine published Argentinian authors silenced by the regime, as well as foreign ones who could not find a home in more orthodox publications. Among the subjects debated in *El Ornitorrinco* were the defence of human rights, the themes of censorship and self-censorship, the absurd possibility of a war with Chile (promoted by both Videla and Pinochet) and other questions related to the role of the intellectual in a climate of terror, including the differences between writing in exile and writing from home. In this latter debate, Julio Cortázar, who had been living in Paris since the fifties, defended the exile's choice as the only possible one to maintain a testimonial presence and bear witness of the abuses back home; Heker countered with a long letter defending the position of the writer who chooses to stay and fight on home ground. 'We are neither heroes nor martyrs,' she wrote to Cortázar, who was a friend. 'One can be a traitor abroad or at home. One can have a national perspective from the vantage point of exile, or write in an ivory tower in one's own country. What a writer has done, what a writer does with his words, that is in the end the only valid question.'

What Heker does with her words is never political in a superficial or dogmatic sense, and yet her world is firmly grounded in the reality of her place and time. The Dutch author Cees Nooteboom once suggested that a writer has ultimately only a handful of themes at his or her disposal. 'There's hunger,' he said, 'there's death, there's illness, there's war. But everything, from the writer's point of view, is political.' Nooteboom used 'political' in its etymological sense: belonging to the *polis*, to the society in which the writer writes. Heker accepts Nooteboom's connotation of political: her characters are steeped in the Argentinian ethos or, rather, in the ethos of Buenos Aires, and in its particular emotional geography, which Jorge Luis Borges so poignantly charted in the thirties and forties.

After Borges received international recognition, it seemed impossible for any Argentinian writer to avoid falling under his enormous shadow. The novelist Manuel Mujica Lainez became so tired with the devotion the younger generation showed towards Borges that he composed a short poem entitled "To a Young Writer."

> It's useless for you to foster
> All hope of forging ahead
> Because however much you scribble
> Borges will have been there first.

Heker carefully avoided the obvious paths that Borges had laid out. The master's fantastic themes, his abhorrence of psychological and sociological portraits, his labyrinths, his games with time and space, never became features of her literary landscape. She admired, of course, Borges' craft and knew, like all those who came after him, that she wrote in a Spanish that had been cleansed and made more efficiently rigorous by Borges, but her interest lay in other things.

Over the years, Heker published a book of essays, *Las hermanas de Shakespeare* (Shakespeare's daughters), and two widely acclaimed novels, *Zona de clivaje* (Cleavage zone) and *El fin de la historia*, the latter translated into English by Andrea Labinger as *The End of the Story*. But even though these are notable accomplishments, it is in the short story that she achieves a kind of unique perfection.

Heker's central theme is the family and its responses to the encroaching world. Also, the curious rituals that couples, adults and children, and siblings among themselves, invent to relate to one another, rituals that, at the same time, help them find their singular identities. The consequences of tiny acts may be enormous ("Now") or ineffable ("The Night of the Comet"). They may distil the creative life to a handful of experiences ("Early Beginnings or *Ars Poetica*") or portray a future life in a single all-encompassing relationship ("Jocasta"). They may entail the loss of everything we take for granted ("The Cruelty of Life") or everything we might hope for ("The Music of Sundays"). They may stem from a quasi–soap opera atmosphere ("Family Life") or from lives of quiet desperation ("Georgina Requeni or the Chosen One"). They may lead to vast existential questions ("Bishop Berkeley or Mariana of the Universe") or to infinitesimal epiphanies ("Strategies Against Sleep"). In every case, Heker's stories raise the quotidian to the literary status of an epic. Her characters face minute dilemmas with the wholeheartedness and courage of knights errant, as if they realized that possible solutions to our greatest sorrows can sometimes be discerned in the undergrowth of private heartbreaks and the tangle of intimate losses, in secret paths that may lead away from the traps of private violence, alcoholism, betrayal of love, familiar misunderstandings. A certain Hasidic belief in the microcosm reflecting the macrocosm underlies Heker's conception of the universe.

One of Heker's best-known stories, gathered in countless anthologies, is "The Stolen Party." The careful building-up of a child's expectation at a birthday party that lies implacably beyond her unnamed borders, mirrors, on a miniature scale, the partitions and prohibitions of society as a whole. Everything can be played out as normal, but one tiny misplaced gesture is bound to shatter the entire social structure. Nothing is said, but the outstretched hand of the 'lady of the house' in the last paragraph, poised in the conventional action of giving, becomes all of a sudden its shadow, the hand of a society that robs children and denies them their right to equality.

Commenting on the craft of the short story, the Irish writer William Trevor said: 'I think it is the art of the glimpse. If the novel is like an intricate Renaissance painting, the short story is an Impressionist painting. It should be an explosion of truth.' When the explosion has taken place and the dust has settled, the reader of Heker's stories is aware that something has been revealed, and that now the world seems both stranger and clearer than before, and feels grateful for the modest miracle.

Alberto Manguel

THE STOLEN PARTY

As soon as she arrived she went straight to the kitchen to see if the monkey was there. It was. What a relief! She wouldn't have liked to admit that her mother had been right. *Monkeys at a birthday?* her mother had sneered. *Get away with you, believing any nonsense you're told!* She was cross, but not because of the monkey, the girl thought; it's just because of the party.

'I don't like you going,' she told her. 'It's a rich people's party.'

'Rich people go to Heaven too,' said the girl, who studied religion at school.

'Get away with Heaven,' said the mother. 'The problem with you, young lady, is that you like to fart higher than your ass.'

The girl didn't approve of the way her mother spoke. She was barely nine, and one of the best in her class.

'I'm going because I've been invited,' she said. 'And I've been invited because Luciana is my friend. So there.'

'Ah yes, your friend,' her mother grumbled. She paused. 'Listen, Rosaura,' she said at last. That one's not your friend. You know what you are to them? The maid's daughter, that's what.'

Rosaura blinked hard: she wasn't going to cry. Then she yelled: 'Shut up! You know nothing about being friends!'

Every afternoon she used to go to Luciana's house and they would both finish their homework while Rosaura's mother did the cleaning. They had their tea in the kitchen, and they told each other secrets. Rosaura loved everything in the big house, and she also loved the people who lived there.

'I'm going because it will be the most lovely party in the whole world, Luciana told me it would. There will be a magician, and he will bring a monkey and everything.'

The mother swung around to take a good look at her child. She put her hands on her hips.

'Monkeys at a birthday?' she said. 'Get away with you, believing any nonsense you're told!'

Rosaura was deeply offended. She thought it unfair of her mother to accuse other people of being liars simply because they were rich. Rosaura wanted to be rich, too, of course. If one day she managed to live in a beautiful palace, would her mother stop loving her? She felt very sad. She wanted to go to that party more than anything else in the world.

'I'll die if I don't go,' she whispered, almost without moving her lips.

She wasn't sure if she had been heard, but on the morning of the party, she discovered that her mother had starched her Christmas dress. And in the afternoon, after washing her hair, her mother rinsed it in apple vinegar so that it would be all nice and shiny. Before going out, Rosaura admired herself in the mirror, with her white dress and glossy hair, and thought she looked terribly pretty.

Señora Ines also seemed to notice. As soon as she saw her, she said, 'How lovely you look today, Rosaura.'

Rosaura gave her starched skirt a slight toss with her hands and walked into the party with a firm step. She said hello to Luciana and asked about the monkey. Luciana put on a secretive look and whispered into Rosaura's ear: 'He's in the kitchen. But don't tell anyone, because it's a surprise.'

Rosaura wanted to make sure. Carefully she entered the kitchen and there she saw it, deep in thought, inside its cage. It looked so funny that Rosaura stood there for a while, watching it. Later, every so often, she would slip out of the party unseen and go and admire it. Rosaura was the only one allowed into the kitchen. Señora Ines had said, 'You yes, but not the others, they're much too boisterous, they might break something.' Rosaura had never broken anything. She even managed the jug of orange juice, carrying it from the kitchen into the dining room. She held it carefully and didn't spill a single drop. And Señora Ines had said, 'Are you sure you can manage a jug as big as that?' Of course she could manage. She wasn't a butterfingers, like the others. Like that blonde girl with the bow in her hair. As soon as she saw Rosaura, the girl with the bow had said, 'And you? Who are you?'

'I'm a friend of Luciana,' said Rosaura.

'No,' said the girl with the bow, 'You are not a friend of Luciana because I'm her cousin, and I know all her friends. And I don't know you.'

'So what,' said Rosaura. 'I come here every afternoon with my mother, and we do our homework together.'

'You and your mother do your homework together?' asked the girl, laughing.

'I and Luciana do our homework together,' said Rosaura, very seriously.

The girl with the bow shrugged her shoulders.

'That's not being friends,' she said. 'Do you go to school together?'

'No.'

'So where do you know her from?' said the girl, getting impatient.

Rosaura remembered her mother's words perfectly. She took a deep breath.

'I'm the daughter of the employee,' she said.

Her mother had said very clearly: 'If someone asks, you say you're the daughter of the employee; that's all.' She also told her to add: 'And proud of it.' But Rosaura thought that never in her life would she dare say something of the sort.

'What employee?' said the girl with the bow. 'Employee in a shop?'

'No,' said Rosaura angrily. 'My mother doesn't sell anything in any shop, so there.'

'So how come she's an employee?' said the girl with the bow.

Just then Señora Ines arrived saying *shh shh*, and asked Rosaura if she wouldn't mind helping serve the hot-dogs, as she knew the house so much better than the others.

'See?' said Rosaura to the girl with the bow, and when no one was looking she kicked her in the shin.

Apart from the girl with the bow, all the others were delightful. The one she liked best was Luciana, with her golden birthday crown; and then the boys. Rosaura won the sack race, and nobody managed to catch her when they played tag. When they split into two teams to play charades, all the boys wanted her for their side. Rosaura felt she had never been so happy in all her life.

But the best was still to come. The best came after Luciana blew out the candles. First the cake. Señora Ines had asked her to help pass the cake around, and Rosaura had enjoyed the task immensely, because everyone called out to her, shouting 'Me, me!' Rosaura remembered a story in which there was a queen who had the power of life or death over her subjects. She had always loved that, having the power of life or death. To Luciana and the boys she gave the largest pieces, and to the girl with the bow she gave a slice so thin one could see through it.

After the cake came the magician, tall and bony, with a fine red cape. A true magician, he could untie handkerchiefs by blowing on them and make a chain with links that had no openings. He could guess what cards were pulled out from a pack, and the monkey was his assistant. He called the monkey 'partner.' 'Let's see here, partner,' he would say, 'Turn over a card.' And, 'Don't run away, partner. Time to work now.'

The final trick was wonderful. One of the children had to hold the monkey in his arms, and the magician said he would make him disappear.

'What, the boy?' they all shouted.

'No, the monkey!' shouted back the magician.

Rosaura thought that this was truly the most amusing party in the whole world.

The magician asked a small fat boy to come and help, but the small fat boy got frightened almost at once and dropped the monkey on the floor. The magician picked him up carefully, whispered something in his ear, and the monkey nodded almost as if he understood.

'You mustn't be so unmanly, my friend,' the magician said to the fat boy.

The magician turned around as if to look for spies.

'A sissy,' said the magician. 'Go sit down.'

Then he stared at all the faces, one by one. Rosaura felt her heart tremble.

'You, with the Spanish eyes,' said the magician. And everyone saw that he was pointing at her.

She wasn't afraid. Neither holding the monkey, nor when the magician made him vanish; not even when, at the end, the magician flung his red cape over Rosaura's head and uttered a few magic words . . . and the monkey reappeared, chattering happily, in her arms. The children clapped furiously. And before Rosaura returned to her seat, the magician said, 'Thank you very much, my little countess.'

She was so pleased with the compliment that a while later, when her mother came to fetch her, that was the first thing she told her.

'I helped the magician and he said to me, "Thank you very much, my little countess."'

It was strange because up to then Rosaura had thought that she was angry with her mother. All along Rosaura had imagined that she would say to her, 'See that the monkey wasn't a lie?' But instead she was so thrilled that she told her mother all about the wonderful magician.

Her mother tapped her on the head and said: 'So now we're a countess!'

But one could see that she was beaming.

And now they both stood in the entrance, because a moment ago Señora Ines, smiling, had said, 'Please wait here a second.'

Her mother suddenly seemed worried.

'What is it?' she asked Rosaura.

'What is what?' said Rosaura. 'It's nothing; she just wants to get the presents for those who are leaving, see?'

She pointed at the fat boy and at a girl with pigtails who were also waiting there, next to their mothers. And she explained about the presents. She knew, because she had been watching those who left before her. When one of the girls was about to leave, Señora Ines would give her a bracelet. When a boy left, Señora Ines gave him a yo-yo. Rosaura preferred the yo-yo because it sparkled, but she didn't mention that to her mother. Her mother might have said: 'So why don't you ask for one, you blockhead?' That's what her mother was like. Rosaura didn't feel like explaining that she'd be horribly ashamed to be the odd one out. Instead she said, 'I was the best-behaved at the party.'

And she said no more because Señora Ines came out into the hall with two bags, one pink and one blue.

First she went up to the fat boy, gave him a yo-yo out of the blue bag, and the fat boy left with his mother. Then she went up to the girl and gave her a bracelet out of the pink bag, and the girl with the pigtails left as well.

Finally she came up to Rosaura and her mother. She had a big smile on her face; Rosaura liked that. Señora Ines looked down at her, looked up at her mother, then said something that made Rosaura proud.

'What a marvellous daughter you have, Herminia.'

For an instant, Rosaura thought that she'd give her two presents: the bracelet and the yo-yo. Señora Ines bent down as if about to look for something. Rosaura leaned forward, stretching out her arm. But she never completed the movement.

Señora Ines didn't look in the pink bag. Nor did she look in the blue bag. Instead she rummaged in her purse. In her hand appeared two bills.

'You really and truly earned this,' she said handing them over. 'Thank you for all your help, my pet.'

Rosaura felt her arms stiffen, stick close to her body, and then she noticed her mother's hand on her shoulder. Instinctively she pressed herself against her mother's body. That was all. Except her eyes. Rosaura's eyes had a cold, clear look that fixed itself on Señora Ines' face.

Señora Ines, motionless, stood there with her hand outstretched. As if she didn't dare draw it back. As if the slightest change might shatter an infinitely delicate balance.

THEY HAD SEEN THE BURNING BUSH

They undertake the almost infinite adventure. They fly over seven valleys, or seas; the name of the penultimate is Vertigo; the last, Annihilation.
— Jorge Luis Borges, 'The Approach to Al-Mu'tasim'

'That's the way it is,' Néstor Parini had said. 'Life's like that.'

The observation was for Irma (she still had black hair in those days and he used to call her his Negra) but on that occasion she paid no attention to the words; it was his eyes that held her. They were like the eyes of a man possessed.

Nine years later, those eyes were also what Anadelia liked best about her father, although she didn't exactly mind that he was a boxer, either. She had seen boxers on the television and been taken once to the place where they train, but that wasn't the reason why: in fact it had frightened her, the way they hit each other, and the faces they pulled. Mom had explained that Dad didn't have anything against the other man: boxing is like a game, she said. Anadelia didn't believe her, but she still liked thinking that she had touched his gloves and knowing that some Saturday nights he was on the radio and that if she really listened she might pick up the odd word from the bedroom, another formidable left hook, this is no longer a fight, my friends, and would be able to infer that all this was being said about her father, although it was much better before when she hadn't had to infer anything because she hadn't had to listen to the radio from her bed in the other room.

It was different before. On the Saturdays that Néstor had a fight on, they would talk of nothing else and in the evening the three of them—Irma, Rubén and Anadelia—would sit down to listen to the radio together; Irma used to bite on her handkerchief and cuff them if they made a noise. Occasionally she cried. Any neighbours who were still awake in the small hours would sometimes hear shouting. If nothing else, Anadelia used to say, having a father as a boxer was a great way to scare your friends. *You'd better, or my dad will get you.*

That wasn't an opinion shared by her brother, Rubén. One Sunday morning he had stopped asking what happened the night before, and it was just as well, Irma told herself, because she'd rather get the silent treatment than have to keep trotting out the same explanations: *Dad wasn't feeling well last night—he shouldn't even have been there* or *Best fight of his life, but they fixed it for the other guy* or *He was up against a new kid, you know Rubén, sometimes it's not so important to win,* while Néstor would be yelling why give the boy so many explanations? He must have been listening, for Christ's sake. But the boy's silence wasn't healthy. On the days after a match he never wanted to go out, even to run an errand.

'Looks like they stuck it to your old man again.'

And it was true: he had lost. Perhaps people thought that in boxing only winning counts, or that being someone's dad means you have no right to lose, ever. At any rate, Rubén didn't want to go out any more: he spent all day Sunday at home, kicking anything in his path, and swearing at people.

Néstor also stayed indoors on Sundays. Apart from one time when he went out slamming the door behind him and didn't come home for two days. Before leaving he had punched right through the window and hurt Anadelia, who was standing watching: he came back on Tuesday, drunk and shaking. That was the only time he ever went out. He spent Sundays at home, sleeping all over the place, naked to the waist and glistening with green oil. It was strange how they had finally got used to that pungent smell of mint and alcohol. There was a time when Irma would laugh about it. Let this be the last time—she laughed as she rubbed it in—that you come to me all beaten and bruised; otherwise some other Negra can go looking for it down in Riachuelo, he thinks his perfume works wonders on me. That was all long ago, though. These days Sundays still smelled the same—they didn't even notice it unless they were coming back in from outside—but Irma wasn't laughing any more.

The worst thing about Sundays isn't the smell, Irma thought: it's the football. And not because of the shouting that sometimes reached them through the window but because of the boy shouting indoors. Excessively. Deliberately. Avenging himself, with every goal he cheered, of a year-old grievance: his father's great hand tearing the picture of his football team off the wall. It's so that you learn, he had said, and to start with Rubén had watched him, fearfully. A son of mine should be prepared to tear his own heart out to get to where he wants, like I did at your age. I got by just with these (and he looked at his own hands as if they belonged to someone else) because you have to know how to stand up to everyone, you alone against them, to show what you're made of. Put everything on the line. And you come to me with eleven poofs—film actors by the look of them—as interchangeable as football cards and who fall about crying if anyone so much as puts a finger on them.

It was like growing up in an instant: the scales fell from Rubén's eyes. He stood facing Néstor, who had ripped down his poster with one swipe and was now calling him queer, and saw everything differently. Who was this man to lay down the law, to him, someone who had to hide indoors the day after a fight? Because you can say yes he lost, so what, once. But not over and over. One day someone or other's going to ask, and not without reason: 'what exactly makes your old man a boxer?' And the insults will come next. That's why Rubén thinks *who am I afraid of?* and holds his gaze steady. And keeps watching him, even when Irma slaps him across the face, to teach you to grin when your father's talking to you. And Néstor Parini has to withstand his son's gaze.

'That boy's gone wrong,' he said that night.

Irma said he hadn't: he was a bit rebellious, but incapable of malice. And it occurred to Anadelia that her mother was lying. Rubén hated his father, she could have sworn as much, she who knew her father better than anyone because one Sunday morning, when she had moved closer to watch him sleeping, he had woken up. That gave her a shock because Mom said he mustn't be disturbed when he's asleep, but her father had squeezed her against his chest, which was big and hard, and asked her who he was, *What in God's name am I?* was the question, and Anadelia had answered that he was the best in the world because he was a boxer. Dad had cried and so had she. Nobody else knew what he was like, least of all Rubén.

Finally Irma had to acknowledge this, too. It was a Tuesday night, four days before the last fight. She had just told Rubén to go down to the store to get the meat. The boy slowly—scornfully?—turned his head and looked at the window. Cold had misted up the glass panes; rain beat against them.

'Well you have to go anyway,' said Irma. 'He's got training tomorrow.'

And she saw in her son's eyes, which were now fixed on her, that there was something fraudulent about these words. They didn't sound like the ones that, nine years earlier, on another night—one that had such a new smell of spring as gave her a wild desire to be with Néstor until dawn—had made Irma understand that wouldn't be possible. *He's got training tomorrow.* She'll have to go back home early and on her own, and without protestations. Because there's one thing his Negra has to understand if she really loves him as she says she does: he's going to be a champion, whatever it takes; life's not worth living otherwise.

Rubén shrugged his shoulders and Irma intuited two things: that perhaps it was true that her son didn't love his father, and that there was something grotesque about all this. Grotesque that Néstor Parini had to eat a juicy steak at six o'clock in the morning and that she had to get up at five o'clock to have everything ready and that her son had to go out in a storm to get meat for the next morning. Why go to such lengths?

'Because he's got training, idiot,' she yelled.

And for a few seconds she was frightened that Rubén would say something back. She had a chaotic presentiment of words that were going to be cruel, wounding and irrefutable. Words that, once out of Rubén's mouth, would bring the world down around them. Or at least her part of the strange, vertiginous world that Irma Parini didn't comprehend but which she had lived in since the age of eighteen, when she had entered it as one enters a dream, love-struck, falling into the madness of others, of men who burn while they wait, bound by an obsession that will either lift them to the highest reaches or eat them alive.

∎

'With these,' Néstor said, looking at his fists, and she believed him.

It's an evening in Barracas. They've been strolling in Patricios Park, the sun is setting and Irma is happy. He's just told her that he's a boxer. Irma pretends to be amazed, though she already knew this. When they first told her (it was a friend who found out because Irma, ever since she laid eyes on him, speaks of nothing else) she laughed the easy laughter of a woman who knows about such things. *All the guys are into that nowadays,* she said, and she meant that they should stop spouting nonsense and tell her something serious about the boy with the eyes.

Today they've been walking for hours and there could be no more ecstatic day on earth than this one, the day that Irma discovers Néstor's hands and finds out what it is like to fall in love for life and decides that nothing else matters, except this crazy boy. Because he is a crazy boy: just a lad. Now night's falling in San Cristóbal and she knows it more than ever because she has seen a side of him nobody else sees. Out of control: crazy in love. He stops on a corner and, even though people are watching, raises his hands in front of his face, challenging the air. A left hook, a blow to the face; shouting to his laughing girl and shouting into the wind that he holds the whole world between these hands and that he will give it to her.

It makes her heart pound to see him like this. For that reason—because now Irma's desperate to throw herself at him, to run her hands through his hair—she spontaneously reinvents herself as a wise woman, like the one who said yesterday that all the guys are into that and means to say it again, this time for him. So that he learns. Néstor walks over to her and she laughs; she's ruffled the big man's feathers—how funny! She'll say it now as though mocking his obsession.

'But what is it with you men nowadays?' Her observation sounds stern, reproving. Righteous.

All of them; her brother too: mad about football. At home they'd like to wring his neck; get a job, they say. They don't understand the way boys are. Let him be, she always says; he'll get over it. And it makes her laugh, her weighty mission to protect the big boys.

She doesn't know exactly when she stopped laughing. At some point Néstor grabbed her roughly by the arm and in that second she knew the horror of losing everything.

Afterwards, looking for him in dark streets, she thinks that it was the way he looked, not his hand, that made her universe explode.

She learns the reason for his reaction later on. They're standing beside a wall and looking down at his hands he says that boxing is different. There are people who don't understand it, right, but they aren't boxers: they're just doing sport. This is worthy of something better, Negra, and if I can't do it, nobody can. I've known it since I was a boy: I saw my old man working away with his plastering trowel every day and you wonder where's the point in a life like that. Not me. I'm going to the top, the very top, and with these, see, with these fists and this body. Because that's what boxing is: you give it everything you have. You don't keep anything back. If you get there it's because you laid your soul on the line. Anything less is Sunday afternoon sports.

She doesn't understand. But it's enough to look in his eyes, which are shining and strange, for her to say that she believes him. Later on a night-bound patch of waste ground, lying in Néstor's arms, she thinks that yes, that world of vertigo and pain that she was so frightened to see in his face a moment ago is one they will share from now on. For the rest of their lives.

■

But Rubén said nothing: just shrugged his shoulders again and went out. When he came back with the meat he went straight to his room without even looking at her; the wet prints left by his trainers seemed like a provocation to Irma. Hearing him sneeze behind the door, she was going to shout to him to look after himself but that would be absurd, *Weren't you the one who sent him out in the rain?*

'What's wrong?'

That was absurd too: Néstor's question at five o'clock the following morning.

'Why do you ask?' she said.

Before leaving, he said:

'My Negra is getting tired.'

'Don't worry about that,' she said, 'your Negra doesn't get tired.'

And nine years earlier it would have been the truth.

■

She went to look at the boy as he slept and told herself no: today he won't go to school. The previous day's drenching had brought on a cold, she told him later; he should just stay in bed. So she wouldn't go to work? No, she wouldn't go; she was going to stay at home and look after him.

'When I'm older,' said Rubén, 'you won't have to work any more.'

She smiled.

And three days later, on Saturday, sometime before Néstor headed out to the stadium, her back to him while she cleaned a window, she said:

'My brother's opening an ice-cream parlour.'

Néstor looked up surprised because a moment ago he had asked, again, what's wrong.

When Irma turned round, his expression was still question-ing, without understanding. He was never going to understand, it was futile; at heart he was still the man he had always been. But there are things that are fine when you're twenty-one years old, or when Néstor Parini is out wooing his girl. Now he is thirty, the age, or so he told her once, when a boxer is finished. That's when you have to throw in the towel, see Irma, before you start to look pathetic. And afterwards? Forget it. There was no afterwards you said, and that was frightening. But it's been like this for nine years. What are we waiting for now?

She saw shock register on Néstor's face and realised that she had been shouting.

'Can you tell me what the hell we're waiting for now? For you to get killed in the ring so you can finally be noticed? Don't you see that you're finished? Or will they have to put you to work sweeping the stadium floors so that we have food in the house? Come on, tell me now that you weren't born to sell ice cream; tell me again that you were born for greater things. To be a laughing stock, that's why you were born. Jumping rope in front of the mir-ror while your children die of shame. Castrated in bed so you can satisfy your coach the next morning. Well go on, it's your big day. Get going or you'll be late. Show them who's boss, Néstor Parini. Like the man you are.'

The door closed before Irma finished speaking. Later, a neighbour would remark on how pale Néstor Parini looked as he left the house. Irma, still standing by the window, tried to per-suade herself that none of that had really happened: she could never have shouted at him like that; in the street Rubén had to be pulled away from someone who said that news of the outburst was all over town; when Anadelia asked about the match, Irma said there would be no boxing tonight and that it was already time to go to bed, and the girl cried harder than ever; Rubén, when he came in, smiled at his mother and Anadelia wanted to hit him. At half past ten Irma put on the radio and, while waiting to get a signal, had a premonition that something senseless was going to happen and that this event had already been inexorably set in motion. The commentator was saying it isn't a fight to write home about. Irma heard Néstor Parini and felt calmer because nothing unusual was happening. Anadelia, from her bed, heard Parini and stopped crying. And Néstor Parini, who, one night about twenty years ago, under a lamp post of a small town, had clenched the fists of his gigantic shadow, vowed to raise himself above everyone else and heard a unanimous clamour shouting his name, heard his name again: Néstor Parini.

And he knew how to win.

In the same way that someone can grasp in a moment the actual size of the sun, and never forget it. With the same simplicity that prompts us, after marvelling from the ground at the mystery of vertical men, one morning to raise ourselves on our legs and start walking. In that same way, Néstor Parini knew how to win. Right now, opposite Marcelino Reyes. Tomorrow, when he climbed back into the ring. Yesterday, in every fight he ever contested. And in those faraway, elusive fights, the ones he imagined on sleepless nights. The ones that he would never have.

Irma, who had scarcely been paying attention, had to bring her head closer to the radio. In the fourth round she said thank you

God and went to call the children. The neighbours woke up when they began to hear the imperious tone of the broadcaster coming through the wall. 'Something's happening at the Parinis',' said the neighbour and put on his radio. The commentator declared that in all these years this was Néstor Parini's first good fight. And Néstor Parini wondered if it was for that, to hear them say that, that he had spent thirteen years punching a sandbag.

Irma brought out nuts. Patiently she opened them for her children, who were sitting on the floor in their nightclothes. She had put on every light in the house. The three of them sat together around the radio, on tenterhooks, not wanting to miss a single word. Rubén explained to Anadelia what a cross was.

'Dad's winning and you're crying,' he said to his mother. 'What is it with women?' And he asked her not to wake him too late the following morning. Because he's got something to do tomorrow. Out in the street. Irma thought how beautiful life can be, how beautiful life is when your husband starts to become somebody.

And Néstor Parini asked himself again if it was all for this. For what was left to him: to win his next four matches against four poor bastards who hardly know how to stand up and to hear Irma celebrating him as if he had accomplished a feat; to hear her in ten years' time telling some neighbour that her husband had been a boxer in his youth. And to know that nobody, not even the dogs, will ever remember Néstor Parini. If it was for that that he had torn his heart out. And wrecked her life. And made my own son hate me.

The commentator said that perhaps this lad Parini could still retrieve his form and give us a few more good matches.

And Néstor remembered his vast shadow and grew to the size of his own shadow, lifted himself to the heights from which there's no return and said, no. Not for that. And he landed a formidable blow right in Marcelino Reyes' liver. Not for that. And he punched him in the kidneys. Not for that. And his fist described a cold parabola, then smashed into Marcelino Reyes' testicles.

The spectators roared their indignation, the commentator gave shrill explanations, Irma put the children to bed, the neighbours told one another that Néstor Parini had gone mad. And Néstor Parini kept hitting, right up until the moment when the referee ended the match.

Two hours later, while a hundred thousand people were still trying to find a motive for this extraordinary behaviour, an ambulance travelled across Buenos Aires. And sometime later, when Irma had finally struck on the most beautiful way to ask her husband's forgiveness, a police officer came to inform her of the death of Néstor Parini. He said that he had thrown himself under a train for reasons still unknown.

'How much longer till Mom comes home?'

It's the fourth time Mariana has asked that question. The first time, her sister Lucia answered that she'd be back real soon; the second, how the heck was she to know when Mom would be back; the third time, she didn't answer, she just raised her eyebrows and stared at Mariana. That was when Mariana decided that things weren't going all that well and that the best thing to do was not to ask any more questions. *Anyhow,* she asked herself, *Why do I want Mom to come back, if I'm here with Lucia . . . ?* She corrected herself: *Why do I want Mom to come back, if I'm here with my big sister?* She blinked, deeply moved by the thought. *Big sisters look after little sisters,* she told herself as if she were reciting a poem. *How lucky to have a big sister.* Lucia, with large guardian-angel wings, hovered for a second over Mariana's head. But in a flash the winged image was replaced by another, one which returned every time their mother left them on their own: Lucia, eyes bulging out of their sockets, hair in a furious tangle, was pointing a gun at her. Sometimes there was no gun. Lucia would pounce on her, trying to rip Mariana's eyes out with her nails. Or strangle her. The reason was always the same: Lucia had gone mad.

It is a well-known fact that mad people kill normal people, which meant that if Lucia went mad when they were alone together, she'd kill Mariana. That was obvious. Therefore Mariana decides to abandon her good intentions and asks again, for the fourth time, 'How much longer till Mom comes home?'

Lucia stops reading and sighs.

'What I'd like to know,' she says (and Mariana thinks, *She said 'I'd like to know'; does one say 'I would like to know' or 'I should like to know'?*) 'What I'd like to know is why in God's name do you always need Mom around?'

'No.' *Now she'll ask me, 'No what?' She always manages to make things difficult.* But Lucia says nothing, and Mariana continues, 'I was just curious, that's all.'

'At twelve.'

'What do you mean, at twelve!' Mariana cries. 'But it's only ten to nine now!'

'I mean at twelve, six and six,' Lucia says.

Mariana howls with laughter at the joke; she laughs so hard that for a moment she thinks she'll die laughing. To tell the truth, she can't imagine anyone else on earth could be as funny as her sister. *She's the funniest, nicest person in the world, and she'll never go mad. Why should she go mad, she, who's so absolutely terrific?*

'Lu,' she says adoringly, 'Let's play something, okay? Let's, okay?'

'I'm reading.'

'Reading what?'

'*Mediocre Man.*'

'Ah.' *I bet now she'll ask me if I know what mediocre man means, and I won't know, and she'll say then, 'Why do you say*

"*Ah,*" *you idiot?'* Quickly she asks, 'Lu, I can't remember, what does Mediocre Man mean?'

'The Mediocre Man is the man who has no ideals in life.'

'Ah.' This lays her mind at rest, because she certainly has ideals in life. She always imagines herself already grown up, all her problems over, everyone understands her, things turn out fine, and the world is wonderful. That's having ideals in life.

'Lu,' she says, 'we, I mean, you and I, we're not mediocre, are we?'

'A pest,' Lucia says. 'That's what you are.'

'Lucia, why is it that you're so unpleasant to everyone, eh?'

'Listen, Mariana. Do you mind just letting me read in peace?'

'You're unpleasant to everyone. That's terrible, Lucia. You fight with Mom, you fight with Dad. With *everyone.*' Mariana lets out a deep sigh. 'You give your parents nothing but trouble, Lucia.'

'Mariana, I wish you'd just drop dead, okay?'

'You're horrible, Lucia, horrible! You don't say to anyone that you wish they would drop dead, not to your worst enemy, and certainly not to your own sister.'

'That's it, now start to cry, so that afterwards they will scream at me and say that I torture you.'

'Afterwards? When afterwards? Do you know exactly *when* Mom will be back?'

'Just afterwards.' Lucia has gone back to reading *Mediocre Man.* 'Afterwards is afterwards.' She lifts her eyes and frowns as if she were meditating on something very important. 'The future, I mean.'

'What future? You said Mom would be back very soon.'

Lucia shakes her head in resignation and goes back to her book.

'Yes, of course, she'll be back very soon.'

'No. Yes, of course, no. Is she coming back very soon or isn't she coming back very soon?'

Lucia glares at Mariana; then she seems to remember something and smiles briefly.

'And anyway what does it matter?' She shrugs her shoulders.

'What do you mean, what does it matter? You don't know what you're saying, do you? If someone comes home very soon, it means she comes home very soon, doesn't it?'

'*If* someone comes home, yes.'

'What?'

'I just said that *if* someone comes home, then yes. Will you please let me read?'

'You're a cow, that's what you are! What you really want is for Mom never to come home again!'

Lucia closes the book and lays it down on the bed. She sighs.

'It has nothing to do with my wanting it or not,' she explains. 'What I'm saying is that it simply doesn't matter if Mom is here or there.'

'What do you mean, there?'

'Just there; anywhere; it's all the same.'

'Why the same?'

Lucia rests her chin on both her hands and stares gravely at Mariana.

'Listen, Mariana,' she says. 'I've got something to tell you. Mom doesn't exist.'

Mariana jumps.

'Don't be stupid, okay?' she says, trying to look calm. 'You know Mom doesn't like you saying stupid things like that.'

'They're not stupid things. Anyway, who cares what Mom says, if Mom doesn't exist?'

'Lu, I'm telling you for the last time: I-don't-like-you-say-ing-stu-pid-things, okay?'

'Look, Mariana,' Lucia says in a tired tone of voice. 'I'm not making it up; there's a whole theory about it, a book.'

'What does it say, the book?'

'What I just said. That nothing really exists. That we imagine the world.'

'*What* do we imagine about the world?'

'Everything.'

'You just want to frighten me, Lucia. Books don't say things like that. What does it say, eh? For real.'

'I've told you a thousand times. The desk, see? There isn't really a desk there, you just imagine there's a desk. Understand? You, now, this very minute, imagine that you're inside a room, sitting on the bed, talking to me, and you imagine that somewhere else, far away, is Mom. That's why you want Mom to come back. But those places don't really exist, there is no here or far away. It's all inside your head. *You* are imagining it all.'

'And you?'

'I what?'

'There's you, see?' Mariana says with sudden joy. 'You can't imagine the desk in the same exact place that I imagine it, can you?'

'You've got it all wrong, Mariana sweetheart. You just don't understand, as usual. It's not that both of us imagine that the desk is in the same place: it's that *you imagine* that both of us imagine that the desk is in the same place.'

'No, no, no, no. *You* got it all wrong. Each of us doesn't imagine things on our own, and one can't guess what the other is imagining. You *talk* about what you imagine. I say to you: how many pictures are there in this room? And I say to myself: there are three pictures in this room. And at exactly the same time you tell me that there are three pictures in this room. That means that the three pictures are here, that we see them, not that we imagine them. Because two people can't imagine the same thing at the same time.'

'Two can't, that's true.'

'What do you mean?'

'I'm saying that *two* people can't.'

'I don't understand what you're saying.'

'I'm saying that you are also imagining *me*, Mariana.'

'You're lying, you're lying! You're the biggest liar in the whole world! I hate you, Lucia. Don't you see? If I'm imagining you, how come you know I'm imagining you?'

'I *don't* know, I don't *anything*. You are just making me up, Mariana. You've made up a person called Lucia, who's your sister, and who knows you've made her up. That's all.'

'No, come on, Lu. Say it's not true. What about the book?'

'What book?'

'The book that talks about all this.'

'That talks about what?'

'About things not really existing.'

'Ah, the book . . . The book is also imagined by you.'

'That's a lie, Lucia, a lie! I could never imagine a book like that. I never know about things like that, don't you understand, Lu? I could never imagine something as complicated as that.'

'But my poor Mariana, that book is nothing compared to the other things you've imagined. Think of History and the Law of Gravity and Maths and all the books ever written in the world and Aspirins and the telegraph and planes. Do you realize what you've done?'

'No, Lucia, no, please. Everyone knows about those things. Look. If I bring a lot of people into this room, and I say when I count up to three, we all point to the radio at the same time, then you'll see. We'll all point in the same direction. Let's play at that, Lu, please, come on; let's play at pointing at things. Please.'

'But are you stupid or what? I'm telling you that *you* are the one who's imagining all the people in the world.'

'I don't believe you. You say that just to frighten me. I can't imagine all the people in the world. What about Mom? What about Dad?'

'Them too.'

'Then I'm all alone, Lu!'

'Absolutely. All alone.'

'That's a lie, that's a lie! Say that you're lying! You're just saying that to frighten me, right? Sure. Because everything's here. The beds, the desk, the chairs. I can see them, I can touch them if I want to. Say yes, Lu. So that everything's like before.'

'But why do you want me to say yes, if anyway it will be *you* imagining that *I* am saying yes?'

'Always me? So there's no one but *me* in the world?'

'Right.'

'And you?'

'As I said, you're imagining me.'

'I don't want to imagine any more, Lu. I'm afraid. I'm really frightened, Lu. How much longer till Mom comes home?'

Mariana leans out of the window. Mom, come back soon, she begs. But she no longer knows to whom she's begging, or why. She shuts her eyes and the world disappears; she opens them, and it appears again. Everything, everything, everything. If she can't think about her mother, she won't have a mother any more. And if she can't think about the sky, the sky . . . And dogs and clouds and God. Too many things to think about all at once, all on her own. And why she, alone? Why *she* alone in the universe? When you know about it, it's so difficult. Suddenly she might forget about the sun or her house or Lucia. Or worse, she might remember Lucia, but a mad Lucia coming to kill her with a gun in her hand. And now she realizes at last how dangerous all this is. Because if she can't stop herself thinking about it, then Lucia will really be like that, crazy, and kill her. And then there won't be anyone left to imagine all those things. The trees will disappear and the desk and thunderstorms. The colour red will disappear and all the countries in the world. And the blue sky and the sky at night and the sparrows and the lions in Africa and the earth itself and singing songs. And no one will ever know that, once, a girl called Mariana invented a very complicated place to which she gave the name of Universe.

JOCASTA

When will night be over? Tomorrow all this will seem so foolish. All I need is morning when he will come and wake me, though God knows if I'll be able to sleep through the night. Just like any other child in the world, isn't he? Jumps out of bed as soon as his eyes are open and comes running very fast, otherwise maybe Mother will have gotten up already and we'll miss the best part of the day. Only at night can one believe something so monstrous; only at night, and I feel sick imagining him now, jumping on my stomach and singing Horsey, horsey, don't you stop, let your hooves go clippety-clop; just a little longer, Mommy. And how can one refuse, Just a little longer, Mommy, when he's playing; who would have the courage to say no, after he looks at you, with longing in his eyes. No, that's enough, Daniel; it's very late. It's enough because tonight your mother felt filthy, once and for all, and now she knows that she'll never be able to kiss you like before, tuck you into bed, let you climb up onto her knees whenever you like; from now on it's not right to demand that mother look after you alone and speak only to you, tell you stories and nibble your nose, and tickle you so much you laugh like crazy, and we both laugh with your funny somersaults. He does them carefully, the imp, so you won't take your eyes off him, and then you forget the rest of the world.

I do what I can. I told them today, I do everything possible so he won't be around me all day. They laughed; you know, it looks funny when you're stuck with me all day, watching each of my gestures, scowling like a miniature lover every time I pay attention to one of my friends. They call you Little Oedipus, and even I laugh at the joke. Little Oedipus, I tell them, gets furious — furious — when I'm in bed with his father; it's terrible. But it wasn't terrible, Daniel; nothing that happens beneath the trees in the garden on a lovely summer's day during a restful afternoon with a group of friends is terrible. Your odd ways even add a certain charm; we can spend the hours talking about you without the slightest uneasiness. Of course, my love; it's all right to want to be with Mommy, to enjoy her; she is young, she is pretty, she guesses our words before we say them and knows how to hold us in her arms and make us laugh more than anyone in the world; and she's silly, stupid, to feel so dirty tonight, to think that never again will she be able to stroke you, or let you climb into her arms. She'll put you away, in a school, the sooner the better.

That's a lie, Daniel; it's the night, you know; it transforms even the purest things; loving you as I do becomes awful. But tomorrow it will be the same as before; you'll see when you come in, horsey, horsey, don't you stop, just like any day. Or did it ever matter? I'll let you jump in my arms even if they keep on talking: But that child, Nora; he doesn't let you out of his sight even for a second. See what I mean? I said. But you kept on hugging my neck and putting your fingers on my lips, my little tyrant. You said, Don't talk, and then I explained, What can I do? He's my little tyrant. Don't you think you should do *something*? I do everything

I can, I swear, but there's nothing to be done, and I pushed you gently, go on, Daniel, sweetheart, trying to put you down. But it was just another joke; like calling you Little Oedipus beneath the trees in the garden, when the hideous part was far away. They're funny words we use, words we like listening to: That child is in love with you, Nora. Or saying to them, He's jealous of his father, the little monster. Everything proper, correct, even saying, But get down, Daniel, you see Mommy has something to do. Go and play with Graciela, sweetheart. So what was to come later would have its place. Because, you know, I myself would have put you down, I swear it. Because sometimes I do get angry and say, Well Daniel, that's enough, and I carry you in my arms over to Graciela. Graciela, here's this little rascal for you to look after. I don't know if she liked the gift. Before she used to play alone, quietly, and now she has to look after you, make the effort of holding you back because you, the young gentleman, of course want to go with me but in the end, thank God, you stay there quietly and I can go back to my friends who are still talking about how strange you are. You see, I say, he has me very worried. I don't know what to do; I try to get him to play with other children but immediately he comes after me, running in circles around me like something demented.

Did you see how he kisses me? One would say he's making love to me, lecherous little rascal, and I must say that for his age, he does it wonderfully! And we all laugh because we are spending such a splendid afternoon. All except you, my poor Daniel; while we talk I watch you from the corner of my eye. Graciela is trying hard to entertain you, but you won't take your eyes off me. 'What a devil, do you think he'll be alright with Graciela? He won't take his eyes off you . . .' Of course; you're fighting to get away and however hard Graciela tries to hold you back, she can't. But, now you've freed yourself; you are running towards me; the respite was brief; you've climbed back into my arms; here you are, and it's useless to try to get you down again. You'll stay with me, growing quieter and quieter, until sleep comes over you, and I have to climb the stairs with you in my arms, half asleep, and tuck you into bed. Goodnight, Daniel. Goodnight, Mommy. But there are no good nights for Mommy, Daniel. Never any good nights again. Never again to kiss you and nibble at your nose and tell you stories and wait till morning for you to climb all over me and sing horsey, horsey. It is useless to wait for daybreak: there are things that neither day nor night can blot out. And today, maybe just a second before taking you over to Graciela and allowing everything to happen as usual, I thought, Graciela, that devil of a child, standing there, at a distance from us. Yes, that's what I thought: Devil of a child. Yes, Daniel, the shame of thinking that, the hate that comes from seeing you make faces at her, this doesn't go out with the light. Because I knew you were looking at her: at her wicked and marvellous eyes, her black strands of hair falling this way and that, her pug nose, her naked legs all the way up to the forbidden place. You loved it, Daniel, you loved it.

My God, why did I think something like that, how did I ever imagine she was provoking you with her charming cheekiness? Yet I knew she was wicked and that she was challenging me. We were fighting over you, Daniel. And she was so far away, so free and naked; alone and something to be jealous of, telling you: I can show you my legs up to where I want, I can eat you up with kisses, if I want, we can roll around in the grass, right there, in front of everyone, because I'm a little girl and you can see my knickers, yes, without people thinking things; they'll just say, How lovely, look at them play, happy is the time when one can do those things; and you pull my hair, you tangle yourself in my legs, and I'll lift you up, and we'll both roll, both, because I'm nine years old and I'll do everything for you, so you can have fun. She stood there so invulnerable, all odds on her side, sticking her tongue out at you and calling you with her eyes: Come, Daniel. You smiled at her. The others were still saying, That child, Nora, is really in love with you, but I saw how you smiled; I knew that in a secret way, a way I couldn't reach, you two understood each other. You knew how to say yes to her, if she accepted you as her tyrant, and she answered, Yes, you are so lovely with your blond hair, your blue eyes and your unabashed way of being tender. So here I come to Graciela, you thought: she and I are the same and we love each other.

You went, Daniel. You slid out from my arms without even looking at me; as if you'd climbed up on something like a bush and seen Sebastian behind the hedge and gone off to find him. It's so easy when one knows nothing about betrayals, isn't it Daniel? One is in mother's arms, the best place in the world, wishing to spend one's life like this, huddled up, letting yourself be loved; one feels one would die if anyone tried to tear us away; and then Graciela appears with her devilish eyes and sticks out her tongue, and rolls around in the grass, the best place in the world. One feels one could live like that, rolling around in the wet clover; nobody could ever stop us from playing together, from pulling her hair until she screams, from making her come running from far, far away to make me fly up in the air; laughing out loud at her faces that no one can pull as well as she does. They will never take me from her side; it's useless to watch us, Mommy; it's useless to feel like you can't take your eyes off me and that you can barely hide it with a smile from your friends when they tease: He betrayed you, Nora.

Yes, all men are the same, and you fake a voice as if you were saying something funny, but you're not even looking at them; you're still waiting for my eyes, just one of my looks to let you know that everything's the same, and you'll be calm again; so I can go on playing with Graciela, but I still love you more than anything else. But if it weren't so? But if I loved Graciela more, Graciela who can lift her legs? And you can't. Who can yell like Tarzan. And you can't. Who can fight with me in the grass. And you can't. Who can smear her whole face with orange juice. And you can't. Who can kill herself laughing at the grown-ups all sitting there, looking so stupid. And you can't. So it's useless to smile every time I turn my head; and to make funny faces to win me over. I'm not amused by those faces; I don't even notice them. I don't see you even when you pass by my side. And you've passed three times now; and you've touched me; I felt how you touched me but I didn't turn around. And I know you make noises for me to hear, and you sing that song about the bumble-bee because I like it best. But I don't like it any more. Now you know. Graciela can sing much better songs, pretty Graciela, nobody will take me from her side even if it's night-time and we have to go to sleep. She'll come, earlier today than all the other days, with more cuddles and more promises. But I won't. And I won't. I'll resist up to the last minute; I'll scream and kick when Mommy wants to hold me in her arms. Yes, Daniel, you want to be with Mommy, of course you want Mommy to put you to bed. It's night-time, can't you see? You must remember we love each other so much, Daniel. That I'm the best in the world for you, Daniel. You can't climb the stairs screaming and kicking that way; don't you see you are betraying me, my little monster who doesn't understand betrayal? Don't you know that Mommy *does* understand and that her heart aches, and she can't stand letting you fall asleep in tears, remembering Graciela? I didn't want to hurt you, my darling. I didn't hurt you, it's not true. You fell asleep in peace and quiet and I'm sure that you're having lovely dreams now. Only I am not sleeping. Only I'm afraid of the kisses I gave you, of the caresses, of the terrible way we both played on the bed till you fell asleep, happy and exhausted, thinking of me, I'm sure. And it's useless for me to repeat over and over again that I always kiss you, that I always caress you, and that we always play, both of us, because my little Daniel must be happy. It's useless to say that little Daniel is happy now and he's dreaming lovely dreams; that he doesn't know anything about his miserable mother's ugliness. It is useless to repeat that night turns everything horrible, that tomorrow it will be different. That you will come running to wake me, and everything will be lovely, like every day. Horsey, horsey, don't you stop, let your hooves go clippety-clop. Like every day.

FAMILY LIFE

Nicolas Broda belonged to that type of people who are cardinally unemotional. It is certain that if, one night, looking up into the sky, he saw two stars about to collide, instead of waiting for the bang he would set out to gather the necessary information. And on the very next morning, after a lot of fiddling with Lagrange's equations applied to the mechanics of three heavenly bodies, he would have reached the conclusion that yes, a satellite launched in the past thirty-eight days and another only four days ago would create the illusion of a crash if observed at the time and place from which he was now staring at the sky.

On the morning of July 7 he woke up because a saucepan or something metallic had just been dropped in the next room. *Every house sounds different,* and for a split second he had the intention of asking himself why the word 'different' had crossed his mind. *I've got to get up,* he thought, but he didn't even open his eyes because he vaguely remembered that no, of course, he didn't have to. He didn't have to get up because it was Saturday or because the alarm had not yet rung. It's true that he had to visit the Computer Centre to inspect a routine tryout (he was a Fortran programmer, as well as an advanced-maths student), but it didn't matter if he went now or later. He stretched luxuriantly and reasoned that this was the great thing about Saturdays: they begin like any other day, and then, suddenly, freedom. Freedom? But he immediately discarded this avenue of thought because it occurred to him that it was asinine to start the day with hairsplitting.

He made a small effort and opened his eyes. The next effort took longer and required a little more will power: he turned his head to see the time. It was 8:30. The alarm had not gone off.

For his third effort—pulling his arm from under the blanket and reaching for the clock—he required nothing at all, because his movement was sparked by real curiosity. He wanted to know whether the alarm was broken or whether he had forgotten to wind up the clock. He immediately realized that he had forgotten to wind it up. He also noticed that the alarm hand, usually fixed at 8, now pointed to 8:30. *Whatever did I do last night?* He tried to remember. He was now wide awake.

The saucepan made a noise again, something like a light tapping that stopped at once. It came from his parents' room. He remembered his father, in his dressing gown, standing on the balcony. Suddenly he remembered what he had done last night. He had been in Segismundo Danton's apartment. They had discussed the complex theory of a binary chain, several women, the novels of Musil and finally the times (long gone) when they used to see Tarzan films at the Medrano Theatre. Nicolas had walked home feeling as light as a bird. He later discovered, to his dismay, that his birdlike condition—the feeling of having the brain of a bird—could be attributed to his having forgotten in Segismundo's apartment a briefcase full of IBM manuals, a dump at least thirty pages long, a rare collection of Maupassant's stories, a universal treatise on pre-Pythagorean mathematics, personal documents, a few odd bits and pieces and the keys whose absence—though not so literally weighty as the rest—obliged him to ring the bell for almost ten minutes and then to exchange socio-economic arguments with his brusquely awoken father. And yet, in spite of this incident, he had felt so carefree and elated that it wasn't strange, he now thought, for him to have forgotten to set the alarm. For the time being he didn't care to consider the question of why the hands were pointing at 8:30. He felt happy. So he jumped out of bed like a soldier and began to sing *'Ay Jalisco, no te rajes'* with all his body and soul. *'Porque es peligroso querer a las mala-aas!'* He held the 'aas' until he could hold it no longer, then he opened the door of his room.

An unknown woman in a lace-trimmed dressing gown—fat, with peroxided hair—was coming out of his parents' bedroom.

'Will you stop shouting?' the woman said.

She went into the bathroom and slammed the door shut.

Nicolas interrupted his song as if someone had switched off his current. *There's a limit to surprise,* he thought. *Over that limit there's inhibition.* He stood in the middle of the hallway, not knowing exactly what to do.

The woman opened the bathroom door and poked her head out.

'Hey, Alfredo,' she started to say, but she stopped herself and stared at him with interest. 'Store's open,' she said, pointing at Nicolas' open fly.

Nicolas rearranged his underwear. He couldn't help admiring the cool head he was keeping under such extraordinary circumstances. He tried imagining the scene when he would tell all this to Segismundo. 'And then an old cow came out of the toilet and called me Alfredo.' 'Sure, and then you both started to sing the drinking song from *Traviata*, right?' 'Look, I swear, there she was, I could have touched her.'

'So?' the woman asked. But something in the way Nicolas was acting must have worried her, because she changed her tone of voice. 'You feeling sick, baby?'

'No.' Nicolas replied. 'No.'

He realised that the woman was approaching him, her hand stretched out in front of her with the unmistakable maternal purpose of feeling his forehead to see if he was running a fever.

'No, no,' Nicolas said again. He arched his body backwards like a soccer player about to hit a ball with his head, turned around, walked away and threw himself into the bathroom with such violence that the woman screamed.

First he looked at himself in the mirror. He needed to think things over, quietly. No, *what I need to do is wash my face.* He washed his face, his neck. Then he put his whole head under the tap. He reasoned that a rational explanation—based on such limited verifiable data—of something as irrational as what had just taken place would imply that he was somehow accepting the irrational. He was certainly capable of not letting himself be deluded by appearances. He dried himself energetically, ran his fingers through his hair and began to stretch out his hand to reach his toothbrush.

What he saw made him stop his hand before it reached its goal. *Five* toothbrushes. Though he could never have described the toothbrushes used by his parents and his brother, he could nevertheless confirm three things: a) they were not these; b) there had always been only four toothbrushes in the bathroom; and c) his own, with the rubber tip—highly recommended for the prevention of paradentosis—wasn't there.

He didn't try to understand. Instead, he thought of doing something more practical: getting dressed. Being in his underwear added a difficulty that it would be wise to overcome. He combed his hair. Hanging from a nail on the door (he had never before seen a nail there) he found a pair of jeans and a shirt. He accepted the fact that they weren't his. *The end justifies the means*, he thought a little incoherently as he was dressing. He noticed that the shirt and the jeans fit him fine.

He came out of the bathroom feeling nervous. He didn't have a clear idea of how to behave, what to do. Should he call that woman? Above all, what should he call her? She had said to him that his 'store' was open. Also, he did have a fever. He sighed and tried not to think about what he was going to do.

'Mom,' he said.

After a few seconds the bedroom door opened a crack, and the head of the blonde woman peered through the opening.

Nicolas took a few steps towards her.

'Lady,' he said decisively, 'first let me tell you that you are not my mother. I also want to know the meaning of all this, and where,' he coughed briefly, 'where I can find my mother.'

He felt one of his eyelids twitching, which bothered him no end.

The woman took a deep breath (she was certainly very fat), pursed her lips and turned around. She spoke to someone inside the bedroom.

'So?' she asked. 'Now what do you say?'

'What, what do I say?' a hoarse voice answered, a man's voice. 'I say that I've been asking for a cup of tea for over an hour, that's what I say.'

The woman took another deep breath, let out a sound like *hmm* and turned again towards Nicolas.

'Look here,' she said. 'Your father's got his gout again. And you bloody well know he's got his gout again. And on top of everything you give me this monkey business.'

Nicolas stared at her in astonishment.

'I'm sorry, Mom,' he said, with such nerve or subtle humour that he was truly sorry that, here in the hallway, he was the only person capable of appreciating it.

The words seemed to have some effect on the woman. She came out of the bedroom, closed the door and approached Nicolas with the vague attitude of a stage conspirator.

'It's terrible, baby,' she whispered in confidential tones. 'Really terrible. This and that, the armchairs, I don't know—everything. This isn't a life, baby.' She pulled a handkerchief out of the pocket of her dressing gown (now she was wearing a plum-coloured dressing gown) and blew her nose. 'And then last night. You didn't hear the fuss?' She paused but not long enough for Nicolas to answer. 'Chelita came home at six; she's a slut your sister, knowing how he flares up. I swear, I thought he'd drop dead then and there. You really didn't hear a thing?'

Nicolas made an ambiguous movement with his head.

'Well,' the woman said. 'You can imagine. I swear, I really swear, there are times I just want to leave you all and run away. Are you going out?' she asked, startled.

Nicolas observed that, with no warning whatsoever, the woman had changed her tone of voice, as if her last question belonged to an entirely different scene.

'Yes,' he said.

'Oh, good,' the woman said. 'Thank God. When you come back, bring me a bag of corn flour from the corner store, Brillo pads, two bags of milk and small noodles to put in the soup. Ask the man if the vaseline arrived. He'll know.'

Just for a second, Nicolas lost his foothold. Then he stepped back on firm ground, like a conqueror. He had determined that, henceforth, he would not lose hold of the situation.

'Can't Chelita go?' he said.

The woman sighed.

'She went to bed at six or later,' she said. 'You think there's a chance in hell she'll get up before one?'

Through the closed door they heard the man with the hoarse voice ask for his tea.

'What did I tell you?' the woman said. 'Sometimes I just want to leave the whole lot of you and run away somewhere.' She pointed at Nicolas' feet. 'Put your shoes on,' she said and went out through the opening that led into the dining room.

As Nicolas entered his room, he noticed that, where the bookcase had always stood, there was now a chest of drawers with shelves in the lower half. He found shoes under the bed. The socks were inside each of the shoes, carefully rolled into balls. Nicolas reasoned that someone who takes such care in stashing away his socks probably always wears clean clothes; he sat on the bed and put on the shoes. He found that they fitted him perfectly.

On the back of a Louis XV–style chair he found a sweater and a coat. Without knowing why, when he saw that they also fitted him, he remembered the story of Goldilocks. In the coat pocket he tucked away two hundred pesos which he had seen on a sort of bedside table, then he left.

It was a grey morning, rather cold. Diaz Velez Street was on his left; Cangallo on his right; the upholstery store right next to the house; the mattress store, La Estrella, just across the road. At the corner Nicolas said hello to the newspaper man, and the newspaper man said hello back. It occurred to him that the best thing to do would be to go home, check that everything was fine and stop all this nonsense. But he immediately abandoned that idea. If everything was indeed fine, the compulsion to return would only have meant that his mental state was abnormal. And if, on the contrary, the woman *was* there, Nicolas would find himself once again in the middle of a situation with no visible solution, a situation from which he needed to escape. So he carried out his purpose to go to the Computer Centre and caught a 26 bus on Corrientes.

He got off at Uribiru and walked to Paraguay. He crossed the entrance and the large hallway and mechanically walked up to the brown door on the left where, on a golden plaque, was written 'Computer Centre'.

He pushed the door open and walked in.

It wasn't the first time he had been aware of this feeling. He had felt it one night, two or three years ago, on his way to the Lorraine cinema. From the moment he had climbed onto the bus he had begun to create and polish, as in a daydream, a program that would allow one to write soap operas through computers. He had gotten off at a stop, which, according to gut feeling, was Parana Street. (His gut had been mistaken; the street was Ayacucho.) He had crossed the road while at the same time going back over his program to see whether he hadn't fallen into a dead-end loop. Only when he was at the point of entering the cinema had he realised that no cinema was there at all, no bookstore to the right, no theatre across the road. *He was in a totally unfamiliar place.* For several seconds he had borne the unbearable impression that reality had shifted, that everything he believed in was false, that his points of reference suddenly made no sense.

The same thing happened to him again at the Computer Centre. But this time he had made no mistake. When he left, sixty seconds later, he had found out something of the utmost importance: no Nicolas Broda worked there. No Nicolas Broda had ever worked there.

Another important fact came to him in front of a yellow apartment building. He had gone there to retrieve his briefcase and to confide his tribulations to Segismundo Danton. He had carefully thought out how to explain all of this to Segismundo, but when he reached for the intercom phone to call apartment 10B, he realised that there was no tenth floor nor Bs of any kind. The building was eight stories high and the apartments were numbered from 1 to 27.

He walked for a long while. He had told himself, somewhat compulsively, that his only hope was not to spend the eighty pesos he had left. But shortly after midday it began to drizzle, and Nicolas was forced to admit that, even though the very idea of going back to that house filled him with anxiety, for the time being there was no other place to go. So he picked out six ten-peso coins and took the bus. Just as he was about to reach his destination, he saw through the window, leaning against a doorway, a large, red-faced man who seemed thrilled at seeing the bus. The man whistled, waved his arms wildly, made a circular gesture with his finger in his ear, indicating that Nicolas should phone him, winked an eye and nodded his head. Nicolas felt himself blushing up to the ears. He tore his eyes away from the window. The lady sitting next to him smiled back a tender and happy smile.

As soon as he got off the bus, a problem occurred to him. Should he go into the store and buy the things the blonde woman had asked him to get, or should he ignore her request? He imagined that if he arrived without the parcel and if the woman saw him, not only would she burst into a rage but she'd probably have him go back into the street to fulfil his duties. To save himself the fuss, he decided to buy the things now.

The shopkeeper looked like the same one he had always known, but he couldn't be certain.

'Just put it on the bill, would you?' he asked, a little anxiously, as the man handed him the parcel.

'No problem, my friend,' said the shopkeeper.

Before leaving, Nicolas undertook one final task.

'Has the vaseline come in?' he asked.

It hadn't. Nicolas hurried to tell the woman when she opened the door, as she was taking the parcel from his hands. He was worried about the possibility of having to touch her. Large women had always frightened him. He felt great relief—too much relief, he thought—when the woman told him it didn't matter. 'It doesn't matter, Alfredo baby,' the woman said. 'Go and sit down to lunch.'

Nicolas went into the dining room and knew them all at a glance. The man at the head of the table, skinny in his striped pyjamas, was the gentleman suffering from gout. To his left was Chelita. To his right was an empty chair in which the blonde woman had been sitting. Next to the blonde woman's place, the Fifth Toothbrush. And next to Chelita was another empty chair in which he sat himself. They were having soup.

The gentleman with the gout tapped his index finger on the edge of the table and turned towards Nicolas.

'Would you be kind enough to tell us where you've been?'

Nicolas tried to think up an appropriate answer, but didn't manage to voice it because the Fifth Toothbrush leapt to his defence.

'Come on, it's good for him to air himself a bit, Rafael,' she said. She had the voice Nicolas had expected from someone wearing those little round glasses. She let out a sigh. 'It's such a nice day out there.'

She winked tenderly at Nicolas by raising one of her cheeks and bending her neck towards the side of her closed eye.

'Fine, fine,' muttered the gentleman with gout. 'In this house everything's fine. If someone spits in the shoe polish, that's fine.

If we're overrun with ants, that's fine. If that slut over there comes home at six in the morning, that's also fine. In this house everything's fine.'

The expression on the Fifth Toothbrush's face changed from tender to insidious.

'Well, I don't know,' she said. 'I certainly don't know how come a decent girl doesn't spend the night under her own roof.'

Nicolas sneaked a look at Chelita and couldn't help admiring her. She was eating her soup like a princess sitting among pirates. He thought that the image had been conjured up by her hair, long and red. Briefly, he saw himself biting it, lying with her in bed. *This is an abomination*, he thought. And then he had a shock. He had just realized that what he had found abominable was what he had been on the point of thinking: *This is an abomination, she's my sister.*

'What I don't know,' the blonde woman said, 'is why you don't stick that tongue of yours up your ass.'

With this, the group became sullen. From time to time, the Fifth Toothbrush would pull out a handkerchief and blow her nose. When she did, the blonde woman would grunt briefly and stare at the gentleman with gout. Finally, it seemed that the gentleman with gout could bear the tension no longer. He told Nicolas to go and turn on the TV. Nicolas understood the role that he (or his other) played in this household.

He undertook a minor experiment: he asked Chelita to pass him the salt. Thanks to a mental effort he had managed (he thought) to recover an ordinary air of 'ironic and aloof man of science.' He felt handsome. Discreetly uninterested he waited to see what would happen. He was disappointed: when Chelita turned her head to reach the salt, she didn't show the slightest recognition of any change in his appearance. All she managed was a quick grimace, as if she were fed up with something. Then she carried on eating. Nicolas felt—never before had he felt anything like it—that Chelita despised him.

After this failure, he refrained from trying to charm anyone. He behaved just as the others expected him to behave, and this spared him any more bother. The truth is that he had very little chance to behave in any way whatsoever, because as soon as he finished his meal he locked himself away in his room. (If it could be called his room, this room without a single book or a single number jotted down on paper; not even the slightest secret cigarette burn that Nicolas could recognize as his own.)

In a grade-four notebook he learnt his full name: Alfredo Walter di Fiore. He also learnt that his teacher had felt certain that, with dedication and effort, he would be able to overcome his present difficulties and come up a winner. The reading material proved to be even less revealing. The only indication of some sort of passion (perhaps simply a question of chance) was a pair of books on accountancy. Nicolas also found *My Mountains*, poems by Joaquin V. Gonzalez; *The Citadel* by Cronin; three or four westerns; one Harlequin novel; *Murder considered as one of the Fine Arts*; a history book by Bartolome Mitre; *Don Quixote*; several special issues of *Fantasy Magazine*; a women's weekly; three issues of *The Reader's Digest*; a botanical handbook for high schools; a third-year accountancy primer; *Heidi*; *Everything you ever wanted to know about Accountancy*; *Everything you ever wanted to know about the Great Ideas of Mankind; Everything you ever wanted to know about Your Digestion; The Thirsty Nymph;* and *Little Men.*

There were no letters anywhere. He found the photograph of a fat, rather plain girl. *For Alfredo, Love, Always.* He also found a pad of receipts with several pages torn out. On receipt number 43 was written in pencil — the handwriting resembled his own — 'love,' 'dove,' 'heart,' 'dart,' and a bit further down, 'Why don't you all go fuck yourselves.'

By 7:00 he had managed to put the facts into some sort of order: either this was a dream, or this was really happening. If this was a dream, was it possible that, within the dream itself, he was considering the possibility of its being a dream? Yes, of course, things like that do happen in dreams. But do reasonings like this also happen in dreams? By 7:20 he had accepted that *this was really happening.* He went out for a walk.

At the corner store he asked the man to let him have a packet of cigarettes on credit. The man agreed with a sly conniving smirk. At the entrance to a bookstore, he stopped himself from smiling at a teenager loaded down with parcels and rolls of wallpaper because he was unaccountably afraid that his smile might seem stupid or obscene. He carried on with a vague feeling of guilt. He heard the parcels and the rolls of paper fall to the ground behind his back. Without thinking he turned around, retraced his steps and picked up the teenager's belongings. 'Thanks,' she said. And something happened: she looked at him.

Nicolas had been looked at as Nicolas.

Only then did he smile at the girl. *You might take all away from me . . . And yet . . .* The quotation crossed his mind. He was a student of higher mathematics, lover of Musil's books, old fan of Tarzan's films at the Medrano Theatre, and he was smiling at a girl.

She rearranged the parcels and the rolls of paper, thanked him once again, warmly, and went on her way.

Nicolas realized that the stars had come out. He managed to find a couple in the Centaur constellation. *You might take all away from me! Everything—the rose, the lyre! . . . And yet, one thing will still remain!* Something in his heart sang out.

It wasn't as if he were suddenly happy, though. Those he had loved, the things he had shared, that which until yesterday had been his past: where would he look for them now? He felt utterly alone. *But he was himself.* And not all the blonde women in the world, not all the gentlemen suffering from gout, not all the red-faced men who lean against doorways would ever be able to dispossess him of this feeling (so like a song, like the happiness of someone singing), this feeling of being himself on a clear evening in July.

He decided that there was only one way out and that he would proceed along that way. He would be Alfredo Walter di Fiore, and he would make Alfredo grow vaster and more powerful than all the blonde women and all the men with gout. He would do for Alfredo Walter di Fiore what he might never have done for Nicolas Broda. Because, ever since his Tarzan days, he had waited for a test, for that heroic or herculean act that only he would be able to undertake. And now he would undertake it.

That very night, as soon as he got home, he took the first step. 'I need to talk to you,' he said to Chelita. 'I think you never actually knew me.' The look in her eyes changed from scorn to surprise, and Nicolas knew he would succeed in his brave efforts. He spoke like an idiot who in the end was not an idiot but in fact had a tortured and contradictory soul. Crushed by life itself, crushed by a family who had pampered him since childhood, all of them, she also, yes, don't start crying now, she also had a part in it—he was fed up and had decided to put an end to all this and start again from scratch. He was letting her know that he was going to study maths. Maths? He, study maths? Yes, maths, he had always dreamt of studying maths, and he was sure that he would make a success of it. He had been secretly preparing himself, he had read many books without letting anyone know, and he was firmly convinced of what he was saying. He was also letting her know that very soon, as soon as he found a new job, he was going to go off and live on his own.

At last she admired him. She felt ashamed and sorry, and wanted to apologize. He didn't need her apologies but allowed her to kiss him and even give him a little hug. He went off to bed as if he'd been to a party.

It wasn't until the next morning, when he woke up and thought about everything that had happened, that he was able to peel the wool off his eyes. He realised that he had barely taken one first step. Ahead lay a long and difficult path.

A great uneasiness swept over him. Suddenly he felt that he would not have the strength to continue. *No*, he said to himself, *I mustn't let myself go to pieces*. One by one he repeated the decisions he had made. Slowly and through sheer will power he began to recapture the enthusiasm of the previous night. It occurred to him that enthusiasm is an incomprehensible state of mind when one is not feeling enthusiastic. He recalled that Weininger had said something similar about genius.

He heard a noise and looked up. Someone was opening the door to his room.

Nicolas saw a tall, thin woman walk in, her hair grey and dishevelled. The woman approached the window and lifted the blind. She turned towards Nicolas' bed.

'Nine o'clock, Federico,' she said.

Then she walked up to a sort of desk, drew a finger across its surface and peered at it. 'Again everything in here is covered with dust,' she said.

Before leaving the room she looked at him once again and then told him to hurry. She reminded him that last night he had promised to get up early and paint the kitchen ceiling.

EVERY PERSON'S LITTLE TREASURE

The inner door barely opened. The face of a grey-haired woman appeared in the crack. Smiling. Ana was unexpectedly reminded of a book illustration. Was it from *Alice in Wonderland?* A smiling cat that disappeared. Not all at once: little by little it rubbed itself out, first the tail, then the body, and finally the head, until only a giant rictus was left hanging in the air. This was similar, but the other way round. As if the smile had been there before the door opened. Waiting for her.

'How can I help you, Señorita?'

The woman's question did not, however, suggest that she had been expecting her visitor. Odd, considering all the publicity there had been, but never mind. Ana put on what she thought of as her bureaucrat's voice.

'It's about the national census, Señora. I'm the census taker.'

'Oh the census taker!' the woman's exclamation was surprising, part enthusiastic greeting, part lamentation. 'I told my daughter that you were coming at midday, but she . . .'

Her sentence hung between them, unfinished. It occurred to Ana that this was a woman who often left things hanging.

'I'm sorry,' she said. 'We come when we can.'

'Of course you do, my dear,' the woman opened the door. 'Please come inside or the wind will carry you off, you're so slight.'

The reference to her size made Ana realise that she was hungry. Or was it the smell? For as she stepped through the door, she was seduced by the aroma of some hearty cooking. The front hall was impeccable. Polished mosaic floor, little crocheted coverings, gleaming furniture; only a comic lying open on the floor seemed out of place. The woman shook her head when she saw it. 'Those children,' she admonished gently, stooping to pick it up. Ana breathed deeply in the smell of cooking, which was stronger now.

'I realise that this is rather an inconvenient time,' she said, 'but it will only take a few minutes.'

'Not at all, my dear. Stay all afternoon if you like! I'm sorry, I didn't introduce myself: I'm Señora de Ferrari. But everyone just calls me Amelia.'

'And I am Ana. Shall I sit down here and we'll get started?'

'I won't hear of it—come with me to the dining room, you'll be more comfortable there,' and she opened a door that led into the courtyard. 'What worries me is that my daughter's gone out and my husband told me only this morning that he's not coming back for lunch, the rotter.' She smiled fondly. 'Poor man, I shouldn't really call him a rotter when he's using his day off to get ahead with work.'

'Actually your husband doesn't need to be present for this.'

The woman coyly raised her hand to her mouth.

'I know you'll laugh at me, and I say that because I have three daughters of my own so I know how young girls think in this day and age—this way, please—but I can't help it, I'm old-fashioned. I'm used to thinking of my husband as the person who takes charge of things in the house, he got me in that habit, I suppose, he's fifteen years older than me. At the time of our marriage I could have passed for his daughter so you see for him I'll always be his—Careful!'

Just in time. A second later and Ana would have stepped on the skateboard that was lying across the doorway.

'Oh those children,' complained the woman again, as she had in the hall. 'You sit down here, my love, and recover!' The chair she indicated was at a table covered with a cloth on which there were lots of cups and the remains of breakfast. 'The thing is he's the baby of the family, you know, the only boy, my little blond munchkin,' she couldn't suppress a giggle. 'We spoil him rotten, as you can imagine.'

Yes, Ana could imagine it. What she couldn't imagine, on the other hand, was why the woman had insisted on bringing her to the dining room when the table was covered in crumbs and there was no clear space to put her forms down. The woman seemed to realise this because she brought a tray to the table and began to clear away the things.

'What must you think of me,' she said; Ana watched impassively as the woman picked up a half-eaten piece of toast and jam. 'The trouble is, with such a large family . . .'

Ana started filling in the headings, trying not to pay attention. Wasn't there something rather voracious about these wives who showed off their husbands and children as though they were minor works of art? When she had finished writing she followed the woman's bustle for a few seconds.

'Don't worry about the table, please. Would you mind very much sitting down for a moment so that we can get this wrapped up? It's only a few questions.'

'I'll be with you in a minute.' Now the woman was gathering up the tablecloth, trying not to let any crumbs fall. 'I hate seeing everything in a mess, believe me, the thing is that, what with today being a holiday, the children didn't get up until twelve. And then of course they went dashing out. I'll just take this to the kitchen then I'm all yours.'

'Señora, please, I still have lots of houses to visit and I haven't had lunch yet. Could we just get down to—'

'Oh my dear, what a monster I am! Here you are starving hungry and I haven't even offered you a bite to eat. Look, I tell you what, since they've all gone and left me landed with lunch, come into the kitchen—come on—you can ask your questions and I'll give you lunch. You'll be doing me a favour, hand on heart, I'm not used to eating on my own.'

'The thing is Señora, that I'm here in a particular capacity,' said Ana, and she felt vaguely stupid.

'Come on, you can't fool me—I'm old enough to be your mother! Come with me to the kitchen, you look famished. My husband and the children love eating in the kitchen.'

Hadn't she been praying until a few minutes ago for someone to offer her something to eat, even a miserable biscuit? Greedily she inhaled the smell of food and stood up.

The woman walked to a door that must lead into another room; she opened it then, as though she had seen something that displeased her, slammed it shut.

'Good God, I was about to make you walk through the bed-rooms,' she said. 'I forgot that I haven't even made the beds today. Come this way'—and she stepped out of the door that led into the courtyard.

Ana shrugged and followed her, what did it matter, at the end of the day. The distant shouts of a woman and a boy's voice could be heard on the other side of the partition wall. The next-door neighbours, she thought. This house has it all.

'They shout at each other all day, it's exhausting,' the woman complained; she looked briefly at Ana and softened her tone. 'Well, they're children just like mine, aren't they? One always sees the speck in another person's eye. Anyway, here's the kitchen—come in.'

A great pot was steaming on the hob. The woman took off the lid and stirred the contents with a wooden spoon. A succulent aroma dispersed through the kitchen.

'Come, look at this, tell me you won't leave me stuck with all this food—there's enough to feed a regiment!' she laughed good-naturedly. 'I always make too much, what can I say, I mean this lot are forever showing up with another guest to feed.'

She's sort of like the ideal mother, Ana thought. She sat down and got the forms ready while the woman set the table for two and ladled the food into a kind of tureen. Finally she brought the tureen to the table and sat down.

'Ask away, dear, then we can eat in peace.'

She sat down and started serving the food onto plates. Ana picked up her pen.

'How many people live in the house?' she asked, although by this stage the question was redundant.

'Only us,' said the woman with a certain pride. 'I'm sorry, you'll want to know who we are and so on. There's my husband, my three daughters and the boy: the little one.' She was silent for a moment. 'Shall I tell you their ages?'

'No, that's not necessary. How many are working?'

'My husband.'

'Only him?'

'Well yes, he supports all of us. I mean, my eldest daughter also works, she's an interior decorator. But just as a hobby, you know. My husband didn't want her to, but I'm with modern youth on this one.'

'Yes, I see. Does anyone go to school?'

The woman laughed.

'What a question—yes, of course. The boy is still in primary school. The youngest of the girls is in the fourth year of secondary and the next one up is finishing Medicine. She's bright, that one, and I'm not saying it just because I'm her mother.'

Surreptitiously, Ana eyed the plate that had just been served. Paris was worth a Mass, it turned out.

'How many bedrooms does the house have?'

'What?' The woman seemed first to brighten and then subside. 'Ah, five. Five bedrooms.'

Ana glanced into the courtyard: it didn't seem like a big place. Oh well. In the box she wrote 'five.' She looked at the woman.

'Very well'—in the tone of a teacher at the end of a lesson.

'Is that it?'

Ana put down her pencil and shuffled the forms together.

'That's it,' she said.

She considered the woman's fascinated expression for a moment before deciding to reach for the plate herself. Unexpectedly the woman sang softly to herself. She seemed younger now: she was glowing.

'So that was it,' she murmured thoughtfully.

Ana ate. The food was really delicious. And the woman could talk all she liked now. About her model husband and her three talented daughters and her cheeky blond boy, the family's pride and joy. Why not? Everyone has a little treasure. Eating made her magnanimous.

'It wasn't that bad, was it?' she asked playfully.

The woman shook her head. She seemed not entirely to have taken in all the extraordinary things that had just happened. Timidly, she pointed to the forms.

'And this, where does it go?' she asked.

'This?' Ana glanced charily at the papers. 'I don't know, I suppose they'll use them for statistics, that sort of thing.'

'Statistics,' the woman repeated, dreamily.

On second thought, it might be better to finish eating quickly and get going, before the woman started talking again. 'Get down from there immediately!' she heard someone shout. 'I'm not going to!' The next-door neighbours: a rowdy bunch, as the woman had said. 'Get down!'

'I said I'm not coming down!' louder now, or closer. 'I want my skateboard!'

Ana looked towards where the voice was coming from. She saw a boy's blond head appear over the partition wall. 'I said get down. You'll fall.'

'Eat up quickly, or it will get cold.'

'I want my skateboard,' the boy repeated. 'Amelia!'

'*Señorita* Amelia,' the neighbour corrected.

'Señorita Amelia!' the boy shouted. 'Are you there?'

Ana looked at the woman; she was eating with her eyes fixed on the plate.

'Señorita Amelia!' The boy spotted Ana in the kitchen. 'Hey, you!' he shouted, 'is Señorita Amelia there?'

Ana looked at the woman, who was still focussing on her plate.

'Listen,' she said with exasperation. 'They're asking for Señorita Amelia—can't you hear them?'

'And what's that to do with me?' said the woman. 'Am I expected to know everyone in the neighbourhood?'

'Can you do me a favour?' the boy asked Ana. 'I lent it to her because she said it was for a nephew but now my mother says that she doesn't have nephews or anything. You're not her nephew, by any chance?' he laughed, delighted by his joke, and the neighbour murmured something inaudible. 'I have to get down now or she'll kill me, but if you see Señorita Amelia, please tell her.'

And like an actor concluding his part, the boy and his blond mop disappeared back behind the wall.

'Have you finished?'

Ana looked up, startled. The woman was standing right beside her. That overflowing quality that had earlier surrounded her like an aura seemed entirely to have disappeared.

She took away the plates and the tureen. Meticulously, determinedly, she threw all the food that was left into the rubbish bin.

All that work wasted, Ana thought. She remembered the six dirty cups, the half-eaten toast, and wanted to get away from the flat as quickly as possible.

'Dessert?'

The face turned to her without expression. As if the woman felt herself mercilessly compelled to play out her role until the last.

'No thank you, I have to go.'

She stood up and collected her things together. The woman very slightly raised her arm.

'So this doesn't . . . ?'

She stopped short. Ana's gaze fell on her hand, fearfully pointing at the forms.

'This stays as it is,' Ana said, very quietly.

For an instant the woman recovered the quality that had previously made her glow.

'Thank you,' she said, barely audible.

Then, in silence, she led Ana to the door. When Ana said goodbye she didn't answer or even look at her. She waited for her to leave, then firmly shut the door, turning the key twice.

NOW

Perhaps it would be best if I go away for a while, if I stay here I'll end up getting agitated. Mama and Adelaida do nothing but cry in the room where Juan Luis sleeps (as if that's going to help my brother in any way) and it's terrible to see Papa: just now I looked into the living room and he's still standing at the window, watching the entrance into our road. We'll know from his face when the ambulance turns in.

It's odd that I wrote *ambulance* because, even as I was writing it, I was imagining them arriving by car. A car would be worse, I don't know why. Actually, I do know. I can't stop thinking that Juan Luis is going to scream like Blanche in A *Streetcar Named Desire*. And they came for Blanche in a car.

■

Just now I told Papa that I was thinking of going out for a stroll but he didn't seem to like the idea. It's not surprising: Juan Luis could wake up at any moment and if he's anything like he was last night, Papa won't be able to manage him alone (and it's clear that we can't count on Mama and Adelaida). I wonder how long this nightmare can go on. But we must not give in to despair. Now that they're taking Juan Luis away, we have to try to forge a new life; we were on the verge of becoming demented ourselves. It seems like centuries since I last felt the sun on my skin.

The first thing we should do is move house. I mooted the idea to Adelaida just now, but she looked at me with a kind of horror. I do understand: our childhood was here. It's not easy detaching yourself from a place. We used to play in this room, when it was the family room, while the adults took a siesta on Sundays. She would be Aleta and Queen Guinevere; I was the wizard Merlin; Juan Luis, Prince Valiant. That crack over there served for tempering the Singing Sword. And in the summer we used to run around in the sun until our heads hurt. But this is precisely what we need to avoid: sentimentality. It's as if everything here is somehow tainted by Juan Luis. Full of his memory, I mean. If we stay in this house, we'll never be able to make a fresh start. Every morning, when Mama waters the azaleas, she'll say the same thing: 'To think this is the flower bed Juan Luis made for me after he sold his first painting, my poor son.' And if anyone points out the cobwebs in the birdbath in the courtyard, Adelaida will say: 'This is where Sebastian tried to give Juan Luis a bath, when Juan Luis was three years old.' And she'll look at her mother and they'll both cry. Only yesterday afternoon, Mama was searching for an X-ray or something and she found that photograph from when Juan Luis won the drawing competition. 'Do you remember how handsome he was?' she said. 'When he came out on the stage everybody cheered. Do you remember how proud I was?' She held the photograph against her heart. 'How old was he?' she asked. 'Ten?' 'No, eleven,' said Adelaida. 'Don't you remember that Sebastian wore long trousers for the first time that day?' Mama sighed deeply and

I realised that she was crying. 'How happy we might have been,' she said. Then, hearing a noise, she glanced up. When she saw me watching from the door she quickly dried her eyes with the back of her hand; she doesn't like anyone to see her crying. I sat down beside her to comfort her, but she started stroking my head like a ninny and murmuring my darling boy. She's very nervy, poor Mama, and she ended up making me nervous too. Or, I don't know, perhaps it's the result of living with this tension for so long. The touch of her hand must have acted as a catalyst, taking me back to another time—I can't have been more than four years old because Juan Luis was still sleeping in a cot in Mama and Papa's room—and I had been dreaming of dogs (or imagining them). That's all it was. A terrifying number of black and hairy dogs, ugly dogs, in a pile, tearing at each other's ears with their teeth. I didn't want to shout for fear of waking my little brother in the room next door. That was the first night, I remember, that I ever heard my heart beating. I was about to cover my ears with my hands and then I felt her come in. Is something wrong, darling boy? I heard her say, above my head. She was stroking my forehead and then she sat down on the bed. And it was as if all the peace in the world settled on my bed, with her.

I suppose that this kind of experience stays fixed in the sub-conscious, waiting for the right stimulus to reactivate it. Anyway it was a big mistake to lose my nerve just at the moment when I most needed to keep calm. As soon as I opened my eyes and saw Mama's face I regretted my weakness. It can't be helped, these things find a way to burst out. I think we could all have ended up going mad if Papa hadn't made a clean break.

Papa came in just now, as I was writing his name. Or rather, he peered around the door into the room, saw me writing and went out again without saying a word. It's incredible, the degree to which people in an extreme situation can lose consciousness of their own acts; Papa must think that what he has done is the most normal thing in the world. But I don't want to mock him; at the end of the day he has borne the brunt of this situation. It can't have been easy to call the hospital. Speaking for myself, I don't know if I could have done it. Especially not in the way he did: I confess that I was amazed by his sangfroid. *Last night he tried to kill his brother*—I heard him clearly. I don't know, I suppose that was the most direct way to convey the gravity of the situation but it sounded very stark all the same. I was lying in bed, and the words sent a jolt through me.

No; the worst is still to come. I mean we'll have to talk to the doctors. They'll want to know when we noticed the first symptoms, what his relationship with me was like, what could have led him to do what he did. And why should I be the one tasked with explaining everything? For two reasons. First: because I have to spare Papa and Mama (and also Adelaida) the trauma of talking about this. Second: because I don't think they would be able to contribute much given that they have pretended for so long that everything Juan Luis did was normal. It's a natural function of their neurosis. Or a survival mechanism. (They did know, however. I remember one particularly significant incident. The five of us were having dinner. A music programme had just ended on the radio. The presenter was reading Guy de Maupassant's *The Horla*. At the point in the story where it starts to become clear what illness the protagonist is suffering from, Adelaida stood up and switched off the radio. A silent gesture, but charged with meaning. I waited for Mama or Papa to do or say something fitting to the parent of a girl who—without asking us—had just interrupted the broadcast of a story to which we were all listening. Nothing happened. The silence that followed was so dense that for a few seconds I feared Juan Luis might pick up the radio and hurl it at someone's head.)

Then again, even as a boy he wasn't normal. Brilliant, yes, but not normal. That's what worries me, I realise now. How to explain that to the doctors. They'll ask me: And why did you never say anything about those strange looks? I'll say, He didn't always look at me that way, Doctor, and when he did I thought it was because he was angry with me. They'll ask: Why did you never tell anyone that he shouted at night? I'll tell them: We were children, Doctor, you know how these things are. I was scared that they would beat him (then Mama will jump in protesting that she has never lifted a hand against any of her children; on second thought, I'd better be careful not to say that and spare myself the complications). They are going to ask: And why did the others notice nothing? That will be the hardest part to explain. I could say: You know how parents generally treat the youngest child, especially someone like Juan Luis, an apparently perfect boy, Doctor, the kind who always carries off the end-of-year prize. Or alternatively: You're the psychiatrist, Doctor; I don't need to explain to you the lengths to which a bourgeois family will go to protect itself from abnormality. No, I can't say that. I won't have the courage to destroy Mama's cherished image. It might be better not to mention our childhood; I don't want to give them reasons to find me responsible for Juan

Luis' illness. We all know what psychiatrists are like—they attribute a significance to everything. I'll say what everyone thinks: that the first sign was at Baldi's house. Nobody can refute that because all five of us were there that time.

We were in the garden, I'm sure of that because I remember noticing the reddish reflections on the face of Señora Baldi (which made her look even fatter than she actually is) and thinking that dusk was a particularly irksome time of day. The talk was of some homeopathic doctor or other. Everyone knows that I find these inane conversations exasperating, so I did what I always do on such occasions: I didn't listen. It's easy: a simple question of perspective. What I mean is, if you consider that a radio has a much greater range from the twelfth floor than it does from sea level, you can understand that it's possible to shrink the radio of one's own perception to the body's compass. Except that this time, when I returned from my isolation I had the impression (to start with it was only an impression, something you could feel in the air more than anything else) that other people in the garden were annoyed. I looked around me, but I realise now that even before looking, I knew what was happening. It was Juan Luis talking, in fact it was most likely his voice that broke my absorption. It wasn't the mere fact of his talking, though, but the way he talked. Without a break, and with a strident tone that made the skin bristle. I noticed that some people were looking at me, as though begging me to intervene. Not Mama and Papa; not Adelaida, either: they still had their eyes on Juan Luis as though nothing strange was happening. It wasn't the last time I observed this reaction or piously contributed to it myself (every time Juan Luis embarked on one of his weird episodes I would tell an anecdote or think up some gambit to divert attention towards me). That afternoon in the garden I attempted one such loving intervention though on this occasion (I must confess) it was totally ineffective, given its ultimate consequences. First, I knocked over a jug of sangria, prompting a commotion that forced Juan Luis to be quiet. Then I contrived to make myself the centre of attention, talking about mechanics, about spiritualism, all that nonsense that people find so fascinating. I'm sure that I succeeded in neutralising my brother on that occasion.

But I don't want any more importance to be given to my be- haviour than it had in reality. The illness was already apparent and, although we avoided talking about the subject, our behav- iour changed. Every day, as the time approached for Juan Luis to come home, we would start shouting at one another, taking umbrage at the slightest trifle, lashing out for no reason. Perhaps not surprisingly, Mama was the most affected. She developed a kind of hysterical defence: finding herself in the company of any other human being, she would start to talk about Juan Luis, about his paintings, his girlfriend, how handsome he was, etc. I mean, I don't want to come across as hyper-sensitive but I sometimes got the impression that she invited people round simply in order to talk to them about my brother. I don't think she did this con- sciously (my mother hasn't a Machiavellian bone in her body) but I realised how bizarre this must seem to our guests—and there was nothing I could do about it. In the beginning, yes, I did try to rein in her panegyrics but that seemed to make her more anxious, so that finally I opted for total silence when people came to visit. (Happily that mania for having visitors seems to have stopped.)

I couldn't sit and do nothing, though. Not only on account of my family (who seemed more burdened every day) but for another, more pressing reason: María Laura. I don't know—I've often asked myself about the strange workings of love. From a logical point of view, there is no reason why a girl like María Laura (the very embodiment of joie de vivre) would feel attracted to a sick man. And yet there she was, as happy as could be and apparently oblivious to any problem.

I tried dropping hints but realised very quickly that I would never convince her of the truth. So the best solution (at the time it seemed like the best) was to go and speak to María Laura's father. I wish I had never done that. The man received me very well, listening to me attentively and promising to do everything I asked but afterwards—I don't know—something came over him. María Laura, perhaps: that girl never liked me. Anyway, the fact is that the man not only allowed Juan Luis to keep going out with his daughter but then he did something even more hare-brained: he told Juan Luis about my visit. No, I'm not imagining it. I know it seems crazy that a serious person would put such a dangerous weapon in the hands of a lunatic but that's how it was. That same night, as soon as Juan Luis came home, I knew what had happened. I could tell just from the way he looked at me. As if he wanted to overpower my very spirit. For a long time he stood watching me, then finally he shook his head. I don't know what he intended by this gesture but it chilled me to the core. I felt that never in my life would I know a minute's peace. You think I'm exaggerating? Not at all. From that day on he began to persecute me. Especially in the way he looked at me. I couldn't take a single step without feeling his eyes fixed on some part of my body. And his words were almost as unbearable as his looks. Every time he alluded to me it was with the purpose of humiliating me. Nothing too obvious, nothing that would make the others think: Juan Luis is a bully. They were subtle attacks, straight to the point. It made me suspect that there was a plan: He was doing *precisely* the things that most vexed me. His plan then was to make me lose control, so that the household's attention fell entirely on me. *He wanted to deceive them, to my detriment.*

The other evening my suspicion was confirmed.

For a long time Juan Luis had been pressing me to let him do a portrait of me; to start with I didn't want to submit to his purposes, but in the end Adelaida persuaded me to go along with the idea; besides, I was interested to know what he was after with all this. When I saw the finished portrait I finally understood. No—it was nothing to do with the painting itself: it was a good portrait. Too much ochre, perhaps. But there was something that powerfully caught my eye: an *unjustifiably yellow* mark between the cheekbone and the right temple. What did that mean? To start with, I wasn't entirely sure, but when I looked up my suspicions were confirmed: Juan Luis was laughing. I could hardly believe what was happening. 'My brother,' I thought, 'my own brother capable of such cynicism.' Blinded by rage, I wanted to hit him but instead I smashed the painting into a thousand pieces. I remember what I was thinking: what else might this maniac do if he is capable of working for two weeks with the sole aim of hurting his brother? What will he not stop at, now that his game has been discovered?

From that day onwards I tried to avoid his presence, but that simply exasperated him. He stalked me, monitoring all my movements. And although I did everything I could to stop him watching me (in these conditions even breathing becomes difficult) I suppose that he had found a way to control me without my realising it. The truth is that every time I tried to do some important work, I would hear Juan Luis' voice coming from the most unexpected places, and I had to get away.

It wasn't so much for myself that I minded, but for my family. For days now, Mama's eyes have been swollen from crying so much, and Adelaida has developed a kind of rash that makes her look terrible. Perhaps it's better for everyone that things ended as they have. I don't know. I have a strange feeling, even though I shouldn't be surprised. What he was going to do was foreseeable. It should have been enough just to see the way he smiled at supper time—the obsequious way he offered me the breast of the chicken—to know that he was embarking on another of his crises. And that this time it would continue to its ultimate conclusion.

But it wasn't at the dinner table that I knew for sure, it was at midnight, when I was lying in bed, still thinking it over. How was I so certain? I don't know. I suppose it was something like animal instinct: rats abandoning a sinking ship. All I know is that I was going over what had happened in the last few days, and what Juan Luis had said at dinner and suddenly I realised that he was planning to kill me that very night. Initially, I admit, I was paralysed with terror but some inner voice urged me to fight for my life. I got up and, barefoot, so as not to make any noise, I went to Juan Luis' bedroom. He didn't move, but I could tell that he wasn't asleep. A fearful thought struck me: *what do I do if he attacks me?* (Juan Luis was always stronger than I was). Although the thought of using a weapon against my brother was repugnant, I knew that my very survival was at stake. I went to the storage room to get an axe. Then, feeling calmer, I returned to his bedroom. From the door I watched the white rectangle of his bed; there was no discernible movement, but he couldn't deceive me any longer. Quietly I approached the bed, and confirming my suspicions, he sat up.

I don't know how far things might have gone if he hadn't seen the axe. Even having seen it, he launched himself at me. Remembering that a person in his state of mind never abandons the course to which he is committed, I defended myself as best I could until Papa and Adelaida arrived and managed to free me.

I must have lost consciousness after that. This morning, when I woke up, I could barely recall the incident. I was trying to work out why my wrist hurt so much when, through the door, I heard my father talking on the telephone. 'As soon as possible,' I heard, 'last night he tried to kill his brother.' Shivers ran down my spine when I heard that. But this is for the best. I can't spend my life hiding away. It's terrible not to feel the sun on my skin. I want to be happy.

■

My God, I think I must have fallen asleep. I can hear his voice outside. Perhaps they've come to get him. I think I'm afraid.

■

Papa isn't standing at the window any more. I called him and he shouted that he was coming, that I should keep calm. I have to speak to him. I have to explain. I had a dream. No, it's not that. It's a feeling I have, that an injustice is about to be perpetrated— that's it. That he grew up with us, or don't they remember that any more? He liked sunny mornings and Prince Valiant. And perhaps, even though we think that everything suddenly changed for him, perhaps within his soul there is still a beautiful and hidden part that nobody yet knows. That nobody will ever know, now. I hear the voices outside. They've come to get him. They are going to encircle him with walls through which the sun shall never enter.

STRATEGIES AGAINST SLEEPING

When the time came to leave, Señora Eloísa still considered herself fortunate to be returning to Azul by car. The travelling salesman—who worked for her daughter's future father-in-law—had arrived punctually to pick her up at the hotel and seemed very proper; he had shown great care in placing her little crocodile skin suitcase on the back seat and even apologised about the car being so full of merchandise. A pointless apology, in the opinion of Señora Eloísa, who always found the exchange of pleasantries with new acquaintances trying. As the car pulled away, she too felt obliged to make trivial remarks about the suffocating heat, prompting an exchange of opinions on low pressure, the probability of rain and the good that rain would do to the country, this last observation naturally leading to the fields of Señora Eloísa's own husband, the trials of being a landowner, the highs and lows of life as a travelling salesman and the various attributes of many other occupations. By the time they reached Cañuelas, Señora Eloísa had already spoken—amiably at first, but with a growing reluctance—about the characters of her three children, the eldest one's impending marriage, assembling a cheese board, good and bad cholesterol and the best kind of diet for a cocker spaniel. She also knew a few details about the man's life, details which, before their arrival in San Miguel del Monte—and after a blessedly prolonged silence—she could no longer even recall. She was tired. She had lent back against the headrest, closed her eyes and begun to feel herself lulled by the low, soporific hum of the engine, evoking cicadas during scorching afternoon siestas *Do you mind if I smoke.* The words seemed to reach her through an oily vapour and with an effort she opened her eyes.

'No, please do.'

She looked sleepily at the man who was driving, whose name she had completely forgotten; was it Señor Ibáñez? Señor Velazco? Mister Magic Bubble? Master Belch?

'A great driving companion.'

This time her eyes sprang open in alarm. Who? Who was a great companion? Looking around her for clues she found nothing: only the man smoking with his eyes open unnecessarily wide. The cigarette, of course. She made an effort to be lively.

'Everyone tells me they're wonderful for clearing the head.'

Nobody had told her any such thing, it had been a mistake not to take the coach back, by now she would have been stretched out in the seat and sleeping peacefully. She half-closed her eyes and thought that she could, up to a point, do the same here. Lean against the headrest and go to sleep. Just like that, how delicious: to fall asleep and not wake up until *a godsend.* Did she hear him speak? Had the man just said 'a godsend'? So was he never going to stop talking?

'. . . because the truth is that tedium makes you tired.'

A joyful spark ignited within Señora Eloísa.

'Unbearably tired,' she agreed. She thought the man would realise now that she needed to sleep.

'And it's not only the tedium. Shall I tell you something?' said the man. 'Last night I didn't sleep a wink. Because of the mosquitoes. Did you know there's been an invasion of mosquitoes?'

Please be quiet, she cried out, silently.

'It's because of this heat,' she said. 'We need a good storm.'

'The storm is on its way—look,' the man nodded towards a dark mass approaching from the south. 'In a couple of minutes we're going to have ourselves a proper drenching, I can tell you.'

'Yes a proper drenching.'

The need to sleep was now a painful sensation against which she had no desire to fight. She let her head loll back again, almost obscenely, her eyelids falling heavily. Little by little she disengaged herself from the heat and the man and surrendered to the monotonous rattle of the car.

But I don't mind the rain if I'm well rested. She let the words slide over her head, almost without registering them. The thing is that today, for some reason, I feel as if I could drop off at any minute. Was some state of alert functioning within her somnolence? The splattering of the first raindrops seemed to trigger it.

'Shall I tell you something? Today, if I hadn't had good company and someone to chat to me, I wouldn't even have come out.'

She didn't open her eyes. She said crisply:

'I don't know that I am particularly good company.'

Fury had brought her almost fully awake, but she wasn't about to give this man the pleasure of a conversation: she pretended to be dozing off. Immediately the clatter of rain started up, like a demolition. For a few minutes that was all she heard and gradually she really did begin to fall asleep.

'Please, talk to me.'

The words burst into her dream like shouting. With difficulty Señora Eloísa opened her eyes.

'Well just look at this rain,' she said.

'Terrible,' said the man.

Already it was her turn again.

'Do you like the rain?' she asked.

'Not much,' said the man.

He certainly wasn't helping. All he wanted was for her to talk and keep him awake. Barely anything.

'I like it, I like it very much,' she said, fearing that this avenue of conversation was leading nowhere; quickly she added: 'but not this kind.'

In a garret, I'd be an artist or a dancer, half-starving, and there'd be a handsome man with a beard, loving me as I had never imagined it was possible to be loved, and rain drumming on a tin roof.

'Not this kind,' she repeated vigorously (she needed to give herself time to find another direction for the conversation: the tiredness was leading her into dead ends). On an impulse she said: 'Once I wrote an essay about the rain.' She laughed. 'I mean, how silly I sound, I must have written lots of essays about the rain, it's hardly an unusual theme.'

She waited. After a few seconds the man said:

'No, I wouldn't say that.'

But he didn't elaborate.

Señora Eloísa applied herself to thinking up new avenues of conversation. She said:

'I used to like writing essays,' luckily she was beginning to feel talkative. 'A teacher once told me I had an artistic temperament. Originality. That essay I was telling you about, it's odd that I should suddenly remember it. I mean, it's odd that I should have said "once I wrote an essay on the rain," don't you think, when in fact I wrote so many'—the secret was to keep talking without pause—'and that I shouldn't have had any idea why I told you that when I did and that now I do. I mean, I don't know if you'll understand this, but now I am sure that when I said "once I wrote an essay on the rain," I meant the beggars' kind rather than any other.'

She paused, proud of herself: she had brought the conversation to an interesting juncture. She would be willing to bet that now the man was going to ask her: Beggars? That would certainly make her job easier.

But no, apparently the word had not caught the man's attention. She, on the other hand, had struck a rich seam because now she clearly remembered the entire essay. This was just what she needed: a concrete subject, something to talk on and on about, even while half-asleep. She said:

'Here's a curious thing: in that essay I said that rain was like a blessing for beggars. Why would I have thought something like that?'

'That is curious,' agreed the man.

Señora Eloísa felt encouraged.

'I had my own explanation for it, quite a logical one. I said that beggars live under a blazing sun, I mean, I suppose that I imagined it was always summer for them, they were burned by the sun and then, when the rain came, it was like a blessing, a "beg-gars' holiday," I think I called it.'

She leaned back on the headrest as though claiming a prize. Through the rain she read AZUL 170 KM and sighed with relief: she had managed to keep talking for a long stretch, the man must be feeling clearer-headed by now. She closed her eyes and enjoyed her own silence and the water's soothing litany. Gently she let herself be pulled towards a sleepy hollow.

'Talk to me.'

He sounded both imperious and desperate. She remembered the man and his tiredness. Could he be as exhausted as her? My God. Without opening her eyes she tried to remember what she had been talking about before falling asleep. The essay. What else was there to say about the essay?

'You must think that . . .'—it was a struggle to take up the thread again—'I mean, the teacher thought that . . .'—and now she seemed to see another angle to this story. She said firmly: 'She drew a red circle. The teacher. She circled "blessing" in red and printed beside it a word that I didn't know at the time: Incoher-ent'—she frowned at the man. 'It wasn't incoherent. Perhaps you think it was incoherent, but it wasn't.'

'No, not at all,' said the man. 'Why would I think that?'

'Yes, I'm sure you do, because even I can see that it may seem incoherent, but there are some things . . .' Some things, what? She no longer saw as clearly as she had a minute ago why it wasn't incoherent. Even so she had to keep talking about something or other before the man ordered her to continue. 'I mean that there are times when heat is worse than . . .' Without meaning to, she caught sight of a road sign. That was a mistake: knowing exactly how many kilometres she had to keep talking filled her with despair, as though she were falling into a well. 'There are times when heat is overwhelming especially if' she searched for the words with a rising sense of panic—what if she never found anything new to talk about? For a very brief moment she had to suppress a desire to open the door and throw herself onto the road. Abruptly she said: 'I once saw a beggar' and her own words surprised her because the image didn't come from her memory or anywhere else: it had come out of nothing, clear against the suffocating heat of Buenos Aires: a young woman, dishevelled and a little distracted among the cars. 'I don't know if she was a beggar, I mean I don't know if that is the right way to describe her: she was fair, and very young, that I do remember, and if she hadn't been so unkempt and so thin, with that expression of hopelessness . . . That was the worst thing, the feeling that she was going to go on, day after day, traipsing among the cars as though nothing in the world mattered to her.'

She paused and looked at the man; he nodded slightly, as though bidding her to continue.

'There were cars—did I tell you there were cars? A traffic jam or something. I was in Buenos Aires with my husband and my . . . I'm sorry, I forgot to tell you that it was shockingly hot, if you don't know about the heat you won't understand any of this. The car was stuck in traffic and the sun was beating through the windscreen, so I put my head out of the window to get a bit of air. That was when I saw her, watching us all with an indifference that frightened me. My husband didn't see her, or rather, I don't know

if he saw her because he didn't mention anything, he doesn't particularly notice these things. She was well dressed—do you see
what I'm saying? A blouse and skirt, very dirty and worn, but you
could tell from a mile off that they were good clothes. There she
was, among the cars, and she wasn't even making an effort to beg,
that's why I'm not sure if it's right to call her a beggar. It was as
though one fine day she had walked out of her house dressed in
these same clothes and closed the front door on everything that
was inside: her husband, her silver service, those stupid functions,
everything she hated, do you see what I mean? Not the boy, she
had him with her, she saw that in reality she didn't hate the boy.
He was heavy, that was all, especially in that heat. But no, she
didn't hate him. She had brought him with her, after all.'

'Sorry, I think I got lost,' the man seemed more awake now.
'There was a child?'

'Of course,' said Señora Eloísa, irritably. 'I told you there was
a child at the start, otherwise what would be so terrible about it?
The woman was there, among the cars, with the boy in her arms
and looking at us with that expression of—. A baby, big and very
fair, fair like the woman and fat, too fat for someone to be carrying
in such heat. Do you see what I'm telling you? Don't tell me that
you do, that you understand, I know that however hard you try
you can't understand it. You think you do, that you understand it
perfectly, but you have to carry a child when you're tired and hot
to know what that's like. And I was sitting down, mind you, not
like the woman; I was sitting comfortably in the car. But even so
I felt the weight on my legs and my skirt sticking to me and then
my baby who was crying as if she were being . . .' she looked with

suspicion at the man who seemed about to say something. She didn't give him the chance. 'But the woman wasn't even sitting down and I think her back must have been aching terribly. She didn't look like someone in pain, she looked indifferent, but even so I could tell that the child was too heavy for her.'

She fell silent, absorbed by these thoughts. The man was shaking his head. Suddenly he seemed to think of something cheering.

'Life, eh?' he said. 'I bet she's the one getting married.'

Señora Eloísa stared at him, perplexed.

'I don't understand what you mean.'

'Your daughter, I mean, it just occurred to me, the crying baby you were carrying,' the man laughed good-naturedly. 'How time flies, she must be the one who's going off to get married.'

'I never said that,' said Señora Eloísa with violence.

'I'm sorry, I didn't mean . . . You said that she was crying and then I thought . . .'

'No, you didn't understand me, she wasn't crying. I said very clearly that she was heavy and that the woman's back must have hurt. But I never said that she cried. Admittedly, she may have been about to cry at any moment. I didn't make that clear, but I admit it now: they all cry. See how desperately they cry when you think they have everything they need and you can't think what's wrong with them? That day it was hot, intolerably so. And the sky was painfully blue, the kind of blue one could be happy with if one were alone or beside somebody very'—she turned her head towards the man. She said angrily: 'If one didn't have to carry on one's lap a baby who keeps crying for no reason'—she waved her hand in front of her, as though batting away an insect. 'The woman didn't make any kind of gesture, just stood there with an air of abandonment, but I could tell straightaway that she was raging. She wanted to throw the boy, hurl him against something, but not because she hated him. She wanted to throw him off because he was very heavy and it was hot, do you understand? It's not possible to bear such a heat, and the weight, and the terror that at any moment they will start crying.'

Then she gazed out at the rain as if she had never said anything.

The man shifted in his seat. He cleared his throat.

'So what happened next?'

She turned back towards him with irritation.

'What do you mean what happened? That happened—doesn't it seem like enough? A very tired woman and with those lovely clothes, I don't know, as if one fine day she had decided that she was tired of everything. Then she grabbed the child, carefully closed the door to her house and off she went. As simple as that. I realize that it's hard to understand but these things happen. One might be perfectly happy, drawing the curtains or eating a biscuit and suddenly one realizes that one can't go on. Do you know what it's like to have a child who cries all day and all night, all day and all night? A child is too heavy for a woman's body. Afterwards, with the others, one gets used to it or, how shall I put it, one gives in, perhaps. But the first is so exasperating. One resists, believe me, one resists and every morning one tells oneself that all is well, that one has everything a woman might dream of, that how the others must . . . No, it's shaming to confess it, but it's true, one even thinks this: about the others, I mean how the other women must envy one with this husband who is so attentive and such a comfortable house and this nice, fat baby. These are the sorts of things one may think of to calm oneself. But one fine day, I don't know, something snaps. The baby who won't stop crying, or the heat, I don't know, it's hard to remember everything accurately if afterwards one isn't allowed to talk about it, don't you see? They kept saying no, they insisted that they knew what it was best to say, that I was ill at any rate and it wasn't advisable for me to talk . . . They put a whole story together, an accident or something like that, I think, but I don't know if it was for the best. Because the only thing I wanted, the one thing I needed was to tell them that I didn't hate her, how could I hate her? I loved her with all my heart. Do you at least understand? All I did was dash her against the floor because she kept crying and crying and she was so heavy, you can't imagine, she was heavier than my whole body could bear.'

Now she was very tired and she thought that she didn't have the strength, she simply didn't have the strength to keep talking for the rest of the journey.

'I want to get out,' she said.

Without saying anything, the man stopped the car. He must have been in a great hurry to get away because he looked at her only once, standing in the rain on the hard shoulder, then immediately pulled away. He didn't even tell her that she'd left her crocodile skin suitcase on the back seat. Just as well, that suitcase was too heavy for her.

GEORGINA REQUENI OR THE CHOSEN ONE

But if I am nothing, if I am to be nothing, why then these dreams of glory which I've had for as long as I can remember?
    — Maria Bashkirtseff

A coach drawn by four white horses is turning the corner. The decorated gentleman inside, astonished at the sight of a six-year-old girl walking *alone and not afraid* along a dark street, leans out of the window, and with a dry monosyllable, orders the coachman to stop.

'Who are you, beautiful child?'

'I'm Georgina Requeni, Sir.'

'And I? Do you know who I am?'

Georgina doesn't know. The gentleman is the President of the Republic, the most important person in the entire country. When the President tells her this, Georgina isn't taken aback and looks him straight in the eye. That is when the President realizes he's facing the most extraordinary child in the world and takes her to live with him in a palace surrounded by gardens. He gives her French dolls and real ponies as big as a big dog, and allows her to wear frilly dresses inside the house. From that day, Georgina appears in all the papers and newsreels. She always travels in a crystal carriage. People greet her with deep bows.

'She looks like a bear in the zoo,' she hears someone say behind her.

Then she wants to die. She, who at that very moment is smiling to her subjects from the window of her carriage, appears to others a rather stupid girl smiling to herself as she turns and turns in the empty patio. From that day on, her mother and her grandmother entertain visitors with stories of how Georgina walks back and forth across the patio like a bear in its cage. When they find her swirling round and round, they call her to ask why she won't play like the other six-year-old girls. *I do play,* Georgina says to herself, *I play in my head.* And then one day she's avenged by the President of the Republic, who orders that her entire family be sent to the dungeon.

How wonderful I was! Georgina feels her eyes glisten. She's thirteen and the memory enthrals her. She takes one small dance step. The window of her room is open, which makes her behave in a very particular way. She lives on the ground floor, and she is certain that some day a handsome young man will stop without her noticing him. He will fall madly in love with the enigmatic girl who does such beautiful things when she is alone. From the corner of her eye she looks towards the window and something happens: a small bird has just landed on the windowsill. Intermittently it preens its feathers, examines with apparent interest the interior of the room and chirps briefly. *He likes me,* Georgina thinks. She feels observed; this troubles and delights her. She places her hands on her chest and casts a tragic look on the bird: 'What has brought you here?' she asks it. 'Go away. Are you not aware that my husband has found us out?' The bird flies away in fright. How very funny. Georgina jumps up and hugs herself for joy. 'How wonderful I am!' she says. 'How wonderful I'll always be!' Today is a very important day for her: about three hours ago, she went to the stationery store and bought an exercise book with red covers. She'll keep a diary, like Maria Bashkirtseff, because there's something that concerns her. One day she'll appear in a book such as the *Wonderful Lives of Famous Boys and Girls*. How will the author know the extraordinary things that happened to her unless she writes everything down very carefully? *You see, my child, here are the lives of all the children in the world who one day became famous: this is Pascal, the young enlightened genius, and this is Bidder, the marvellous little mathematician, and this is Metastasio, the infant troubadour of Rome, and this is Georgina Requeni, the girl who . . .* The world collapses around her. She is already almost fourteen years old, and she still doesn't know what she's going to be. Her father has promised her that when she turns fifteen she'll be able to take classes of Elocution and Dramatic Art with the teacher who lives on Santander Street, but that is a long time away. Sometimes she remembers that at the age of seven Mozart dazzled a prince, then she feels like ending it all and throwing herself out of a window. But she lives on the ground floor, she's out of her mind, she'll be famous and the world will love her. She looks at herself in the mirror. *And I will also be very beautiful.* She lifts her hair, lets it fall over one eye, half-lowers her eyelids, sees a pimple on her chin and wrinkles her nose, oh well, she'll be very beautiful and have lovers, thousands of lovers strewn at her feet. How they'll suffer because of her! *No, dear Sir, don't do it! Don't kill yourself for my sake!* The man kills himself; she is dancing in front of the mirror. She doesn't know what is happening to her; what she does know is that no one, ever, was as happy as this. She goes up to her image and gives it a kiss. This makes her laugh out loud. She runs to the window and looks up at the sky. 'God is blue,' she whispers. The November air, the smell of leaves, of tides; she wants to hug someone very hard and tell him all about her. No, there'll be no need to talk; he'll look her in the eyes and know everything, the tragedies she's been through, her fears, the incredible things she still must do. *My God, life is so wonderful.* Then she makes up her mind: today is the day to begin. It's been almost a year since she bought the exercise book. Since she bought it, she's been waiting for the perfect moment; she believes that every event should be made up of *perfect moments.* She goes to the night table, opens the small drawer and takes out the exercise book with the red covers. She sits at her desk, and with coloured crayons, she writes on the first page: *The Diary of Georgina Requeni.* Then she turns the page, takes her fountain pen and writes, *'I'm fourteen years old. No one can know the feelings in my heart. My heart is wild, and on this day, the whole world is like my heart. Yes! I feel as if my life is going to be wonderful. I feel.'* She stops because she doesn't know how to carry on. She reads what she has written, and she approves.

Now she reads it again as if she were another fourteen-year-old girl reading the words she has written. The other girl can't believe that, at her same age, someone wrote such beautiful lines and cries over the diary which has become a book with Georgina's picture on the cover. The whole world is crying. She has died. Hidden among piles of paper, they have found the exercise book with the red covers, the confession of so many thwarted ideals. It doesn't seem possible that someone like her should die at the dawn of so much promise, she who could have soared so high. Georgina blows her nose, she's such a fool. She crosses out the last '*I feel*' and writes '*I wish.*' '*I wish to soar very, very high.*'

Amazing. She rereads the last sentence, she is truly impressed. For the past two hours she has been trying to get started on what is for her one of the most terrifying jobs in the world: sorting out her papers. She is eighteen and says that sorting out your drawers is like cleaning out your soul. Her soul is full of astounding junk, tatters of stories, but she only needs to rescue whatever is concerned with the relentless destiny she has chosen for herself. She hates being sentimental; she knows that the chosen ones are cold and strong; she has read a lot. The exercise book with the red covers is a real find. She has opened it on the first page and has felt that God is speaking in her ear. The wish to soar very high, amazing; only those who've been predestined can write a sentence like that at the age of fourteen. For an instant she can imagine the exercise book, under a glass cover, in the Museum of the Theatre Arts. She turns the pages but nothing. Here, on the very first page, the diary ends. A few lines of verse copied out, the drawing of a large heart with her name and another name pierced by an arrow, some notes taken in class, and no more. How unsettled one was at fourteen, she thinks with adult insight. She smiles. She has remembered the absurd idea she had that day when she thought of starting the diary. Heroic and premature deaths! At eighteen, she has understood that true heroics lie in the act of living. She rolls up the exercise book and throws it into the garbage. It is like a signal.

With unaccustomed energy, she spills out the contents of drawers, throws papers away and tears faded photos of once fashionable stars off the wall. She sighs with relief: now everything is in order. Now she can, at last, do what she has been promising herself she will do all afternoon. She takes a huge poster with the portrait of Sarah Bernhardt and fixes it to the wall with four thumbtacks. The two women stare at each other. Now Georgina knows what she wants.

'You want me,' he says. 'It's as simple as that.'

They are leaning against the riverside wall, waiting for the sun to come up. Georgina sighs with resignation and somewhat loudly, because she's just realized that Manuel has not understood a single word of what she has been saying. Very carefully she begins to smooth out a green and golden candy wrapper. 'No,' she says. Yes, of course she wants him, she loves him, but it's something else. Theatre, of course. Something else.

'Why something else?' Manuel asks, but a ship's foghorn is heard in the distance.

Georgina has finished smoothing out the wrapper and now rolls it around her index finger. He looks at her hands.

'What will you do?' he asks.

Her face brightens.

'Well,' she replies, 'it's all a bit complicated, I don't know. I could just tell you that I'm going to be a great actress, but it's something more, I don't know how to explain it.'

'No,' he shakes his head. 'With the candy wrapper. I mean what are you going to do *with the candy wrapper?*'

'Ah,' she stares at her finger. 'A little cup. Daddy always used to make one for me. You twist the paper here, then you take out your finger and there: see?'

Manuel pushes the hair away from her face.

'Georgina,' he says. 'Why *something else?*'

She lifts her eyebrows with a look of surprise. 'Theatre, I mean. Why does it have to be something else?'

She laughs and points a finger at him.

'He's jealous,' she says in a singsong. 'Manuel is jealous.' She looks at him in the face and becomes serious. 'Not at all, you fool. It is the same thing. Love, theatre and . . . I don't know how to explain, it's as if I were fated. I mean, as if with everything I do, I'm supposed to rise higher and higher . . . Who knows? To be in decline must be something terrible. Haven't you ever thought about that? I'm always thinking about these things, it's awful.'

Manuel whistles admiringly.

'It's true,' says Georgina. 'The problem is that you don't take me seriously, but that's how it is. What's more, long before I turn into one of those old actresses who go on living God-knows-why—' She stops and looks at him with determination. 'I'll kill myself,' she says.

Manuel puts his palms together and mimics a jump into the river.

'Splash,' he says.

No, no, Georgina shakes her head desperately. *Not in the river, what a philistine, he doesn't understand a thing.* She's talking to him about a luminous ascent towards the loftiest heights, she means putting an end to all, cleanly, at the very top, and he comes out with something as unaesthetic as drowning oneself. Virginia Woolf, of course, but does he imagine her a few moments before the end, thrashing about and swallowing water and probably retching? And then what? A bloated half-rotten corpse drying out on a slab in the morgue. Lovely posthumous image. No, never, nothing like that. A beautiful death, Georgina means. Like her life.

He has watched her as she speaks. Lightly, he touches the tip of her nose.

'Do me a favour,' he says. 'Don't ever kill yourself.'

They can't bear persistence, she thinks from high above a pedestal.

'But yes, you fool. Don't you realize?' she says. 'They must remember me beautiful. Beautiful for ever and ever.'

As soon as the words are out, she has the disagreeable impression of having said too much. She glares at Manuel and then covers her face with her hands.

'No, not now, what an idiot you are,' she says. 'At six in the morning anyone looks awful,' as she uncovers her face and places her hands on her hips, aggressively. 'Anyway, I'm twenty, right? I still have my whole life to get what I want.'

'Get what?' he asks.

'Everything.'

Manuel arches his eyebrows. He sits on the wall. Georgina stands as if waiting for something, and then finally she sits down as well. They sit with their legs dangling towards the river, the sun is about to rise and *all is well*.

'See, that's what I was telling you,' Georgina says. 'We come into the world with these things, who knows why. Strange, isn't it? Imagine: I was only fourteen and already I wrote it down on the very first page of my diary.'

Manuel slaps his forehead with a wide open palm.

'No!' he says. 'Don't tell me that you also keep a diary!'

Georgina is about to explain something to him. She shrugs.

'Of course,' she says.

'Of course?' he laughs. 'Women are out of this world. Okay, tell me.'

'Tell you what? What have women to do with this?'

'What you write in your diary, all that stuff. Let's see if I can finally get to understand you.'

Georgina pulls a face as if she's bothered: curiosity seems to her an unworthy and irritating sentiment. She can't imagine Ibsen worrying about what people write in their diaries.

'Well . . . I don't know,' she says. 'It makes no sense if you tell it.'

'Tell what?'

Georgina turns around, her feet on the wall. The sun has started to come out, and the glimmer hurts her eyes. She crumples the green and golden cup, makes it into a ball and throws it into the water. Then she regrets having done it: Manuel mustn't believe that something has put her in a bad mood. It's a good thing the sun is coming out: they've been on the riverside for an hour now waiting for it to rise. And it does. The sky is blue, red and yellow. That's good.

She turns and sits as before.

'I don't know where to start,' she says. 'Because it turned out to be a very long diary. I would write in it every day . . . And there was always something to write about. I was a terrific adolescent, you know. I mean it, don't laugh. I mean the theatre and all that. I was always talking about the theatre, and about the actress I was going to become. About my idols and about how I was going to work harder and harder until I'd be even greater than all my idols . . . Because unless you reach the highest peaks, life has no sense at all . . . I would also write about that, of course. And my thoughts about life, about fate . . . I don't know . . . that one's fate isn't written down anywhere. I mean, there's no star carrying a sign saying "Georgina Requeni Will Be The Greatest." That's it, you make up your own fate; that's the thing. See my hand? Look! Even the lines of your hand change. *You* change them, see? Really, a palmreader explained it to me once . . . So, well, that's what I wrote about. I felt, I don't know—' She stops and looks at him. 'Happy now?' she asks.

He is about to speak. She anticipates what he is about to ask.

'It was a beautiful diary,' she says. Then, in a mysterious tone, she adds, 'The ceremony was really impressive.'

'Ceremony?' he asks. 'What ceremony?'

His expression is very funny. Georgina is about to laugh.

'The ceremony,' she says. 'Death. Everything must have its ceremony.' She laughs like someone who has just remembered something hilarious. 'You know what I did when I was eighteen?' she asks.

He shakes his head.

'I wrote the last page,' Georgina is glowing. 'A fabulous page, you should have seen. In my opinion, the best page in the entire diary, I mean it . . . The days of small gestures were over; one couldn't help it. Now was the beginning of the real struggle . . . I didn't cry or anything like that. I put the diary on a blue tray. A tray with little angels painted on it, I'll show it to you when you come to the house. I lit a match and *pfff*. It became a blazing bonfire. I stared at it for as long as it took, and then the ashes . . . I bet you can't guess? I threw them to the wind. Don't laugh . . . Just a game, I know. But wasn't it a beautiful ending?'

Manuel looks at her and says nothing. She's in despair because she can't figure out whether he's truly moved (and by what) or whether he's making fun of her.

'I mean it,' she says. 'Everything must end in the same way it lived. What else could I have done? Thrown it into the garbage?'

Imposter, she thinks. *A Hedda Gabler who shoots herself then throws kisses around is an imposter.* Doesn't anyone notice? No one notices. The applause increases, followed by an ovation. Georgina must admit that, speaking in general terms, the public is stupid: they call out the name of the star because they are fans, not because they understand anything about the theatre. The young woman on the proscenium throws one last kiss with an ample movement of the arm. Georgina, back in the wings with the rest of the cast, sees only her back but imagines her starlet's smile. She looks at the woman's nape with scorn. Now Doctor Tesman and Councillor Brack advance and stand on both sides of Hedda Gabler. A new wave of applause; the two actors bow their heads slightly. Now: this is the moment when they are all meant to come forward. What for? Hear them clap, no need to take a bow. The applause becomes weaker. What do they expect? A miracle? Georgina would have liked to know how Sarah Bernhardt herself would have managed to make something decent out of the role of Berta. *Yes, Madam. It's morning already, Madam. Councillor Brack is here to see you, Madam.* No, she can't take it any longer. Today she'll give it all up. She thinks about it hard, as hard as a tombstone, and the clearness of her decision makes her feel better. She's certain that only a privileged spirit is able to be as inflexible as she is: the spirit of a great artist. She lifts her eyes and smiles haughtily at the public. *Dear Lord*, she thinks. *Grant them a minute of greatness to allow them to understand this smile.* The curtain falls for the last time. Georgina heads for the dressing-rooms. She feels that one day, this too will be part of her history. Alone and unknown at the age of twenty-four, making her way through a throng of people who embrace and congratulate one another and ignore her, crossing dark corridors without paying attention to anything, without greeting anyone, without thinking about anything except—

'Oh no, it never concerned me,' she'd smile condescendingly. With exquisite good manners, she'd overlook the fact that several young men, out of sheer admiration, have brought up the subject of her nebulous beginnings.

'But it was something outrageous. A talent like yours . . . Wasted on unbearable minor roles. How were you able to put up with it? Did the thought of giving it all up ever cross your mind?'

'Never,' she'd answer indignantly. 'Do you think that with displays of false pride I'd have become who I am? Learn the lesson well, my children: nothing, nothing at all is ever achieved without struggle. One must start from the bottom, bear every blow and never falter.'

How true! she thinks, reaching the end of the corridor. She has at last understood the meaning of this moment, the greatness locked in all those anonymous years. She opens the door to her dressing-room. The other two women have taken off their costumes. The last performance of the *Three-Penny Opera* is over. In their slips, the two women, both perched on the only chair in the room, are smoking cigarettes. Georgina sees them, steps back and closes the door.

'Come in,' she hears. 'If we try, all three of us can fit.'

Inside the room, they laugh.

'What can you do,' she hears. 'The inconvenience of not being a star.'

Georgina makes a grimace of distaste.

'Let her be,' she hears. 'That's how she is.'

'How?' Georgina cries. '*How* am I?'

Santiago, his back towards her, lying by her side in the bed, isn't startled. In the seven years he has known her, he has learnt not to be bothered by her sudden questions.

'You're Georgina,' he says simply.

'Yes,' she says. 'But. I don't know. I don't know how to explain.'

She remains silent for a moment. Then she says, 'Why are you here, with me?'

He laughs half-heartedly.

'Don't you think it's a bit late in the day to ask me that?'

'You don't understand,' Georgina says. 'In the early days . . . Don't you see? In the early days it was different. It was . . . I don't know. There was a time when everything was crazy, vertiginous. Each time we were together it was something new, something unpredictable. The joy of sin, remember? As if we had things to teach, as if. It was so lovely, Santiago. So lovely. Wasn't it? It was. Wasn't it? It was as I just said, yes? Santiago? Was it?'

He's silent. He looks up at the ceiling and smokes. He seems eternally tired. Or sad.

Georgina speaks again. Her voice is anxious and afraid.

'Was it like that? Tell me, Santiago. Was it?'

Santiago touches her hair.

'Yes, Georgina, yes,' he says.

'I too, you know,' Georgina says. 'I too always felt that way and would think, I don't know, would think, please don't laugh, that every day I'd be more beautiful and more, I don't know, and then. Of course, it's so absurd if you say it yourself, but that's how it is, understand? I thought one day we'd die of too much love.'

Santiago laughs, but it is not a happy laugh.

'Don't laugh. As with all the rest, you know. But I don't. Now . . . Of course, nothing can be repeated. Isn't there . . . ? Isn't there anything, Santiago? How am I?'

'It's okay, Georgina. It's okay. Be quiet.'

'No, no. It's awful. As if I were denying myself, don't you see? Sinking. You know what I should do now if I were the way I imagined myself? You know what? I should say, Goodbye Santiago, goodbye my love, it was all very beautiful but it's all over now for Georgina. And put an end to it all.'

The silence that follows frightens her. She doesn't dare move. At last, he puts his hand on her waist. She relaxes, it's fine. Now everything will be the way it was. And it will be beautiful. Won't it be beautiful? Words are such nonsense. She feels a great calm. This is not being vulnerable, no, it's all right, everything is all right like this.

He still has his hand on Georgina's waist but makes no movement, says nothing. This troubles her. She sighs and curls up against Santiago, suddenly tender and fragile. She laughs.

'I'm a fool,' she says. 'Words are so foolish, you know. Don't ever believe what I say, Santiago. Never believe anything I say.'

He lifts his hand away. Then, with so little violence that the change of position seems rather a thought than an act, he draws away from Georgina.

'No,' Georgina says. 'Why? Everything's okay, silly. Everything will always be okay.'

Santiago is barely smiling. Georgina speaks again: he must believe her when she says it's all a lie.

'That's it,' he says. 'That's exactly it. You've got to understand.'

Before leaving, he touches her face. Georgina sees him leave, without making sense of what is happening.

'Go!' she shouts. 'I never want to see you again, you heartless man!'

Then the door slams shut. The part is over.

Another of the extras, a rather fat man with a stupid face, stares at her inquisitively.

'Why did you make that grimace?' he asks.

'Grimace?' Georgina looks at him with studied indifference. 'When?'

'Just now,' the man says. 'As you closed the door.'

'It wasn't a grimace,' Georgina says, reflecting that the tone of her voice had been far more violent than what the scene called for. 'I was laughing.'

'Ah.'

The man yawns. He plays with the signet ring on his finger.

Georgina waits a few seconds, impatient and uncomfortable not to be asked anything.

'Because once, years ago,' she laughs inexplicably, 'What madness. I kicked a man out, with more or less the same gesture.'

A model in a leotard crosses the studio.

The man follows her with his eyes.

'Yes, of course,' he says.

'I loved him, you know.' Georgina shrugs. 'And all the same, I kicked him out.'

The woman in the leotard turns. She balances a tin of wax in her hand. The man watches her, amused.

'Really,' he says.

'No,' Georgina says. 'No need to be surprised. It was necessary.'

Now the woman in the leotard is half hidden by a gigantic pudding made out of cardboard. The man stares down at his shoes. Georgina follows his stare. They're horrible shoes, an indefinite mustard colour. She wonders what would make a human being choose such ugly shoes.

'You can't understand, can you?' she asks. 'Of course you can't understand. Life in the theatre, you know.' She looks up at the man guardedly. 'It demands many sacrifices.'

The man chuckles softly.

'That's rich,' he says. 'People like us.' He looks at the front of his shirt. He chuckles again. 'That's really rich.'

Georgina looks at her nails.

'How could an idiot understand,' she says.

The man does nothing in particular. He looks around the studio at the TV cameras, the sets. Then he looks at Georgina.

'How old are you?' he asks.

Georgina lifts her head, as if in defiance.

'Thirty-four,' she replies.

Now the man stares at her from head to foot.

'You're still young,' he says.

A blow. As if the meaning of the words were exactly the opposite. *I shouldn't mix with people like that.* Georgina is about to explain something, but the man is no longer there. She shrugs and goes out into the street. It's a cold, bright night. Momentarily, she feels relieved. *I can't bear this life.* She's startled. *No: it's just the noise. I was never able to bear it.* She lifts her head haughtily. *Nothing so distant from art as all this stupid cackling, yes sir.* She doesn't realize how fast she's walking. A man with a little feather in his hat says something to her that she doesn't quite understand. She feels a sweet sensation of pleasure. *I'm still young,* she thinks. But as soon as she has the thought, she's overcome by uneasiness.

Someone once said these words to her. When? Oh well, better not think about it. The man in the hat wasn't old. Everything's fine once again, isn't it? Of course it is. After all, no one ever said it was going to be easy. What matters is carrying on: reaching the end without stopping. One day, they'll know the whole truth. *The Memoirs of.* Of course it was difficult, but one had to keep climbing. Higher, understand? Higher and higher each time. So that life itself becomes one luminous ascent. That's something you carry within, do you hear? It's as if a light had been lit somewhere inside.

Georgina laughs, ecstatic. It's been a while since she's felt so joyful. The young men laugh with her. One of them fills her glass again; this promises to be a night of great rejoicing. Guitar music, young poets, meat rolls and gallons of wine. The noise doesn't allow one to listen very carefully, can you hear? As if one were God and forced to do everything. The hand, look, even the lines of the hand can be changed. Through sheer will. Will to be beautiful, will to be great. Because nothing is written, don't you realise, destiny isn't written on a star, and where, where does it say that Georgina Requeni will be a great actress, will be beautiful?

Joy! Joy! There's much laughter here, many young voices. *Another samba,* they say. *I love you. More wine. Have you noticed? Have you noticed there's always an old bag getting pissed at these parties?* But Georgina can't make out the voices very clearly and goes on laughing, drinking wine, talking. Because there's no Santiago, there's no one to tell her to shut up, to tell her everything's fine, to tell her she's fumbling over the words and is about to fall down. 'Never fall, never ever fall,' she says. Because a woman grown old is a monster. And before reaching that stage, Georgina will kill herself.

Now they're no longer laughing. 'It's pathetic,' they're saying. And also that life is cruel.

And Georgina Requeni, who is still holding her hand in front of her and has just shouted something, even though she can't remember what, looks around, terrified, as if her own cry had woken her and sees, as one sees the end of a dream, that all the faces are strange and are staring at her. And that the hand stretched out in front of her is the hand of an old woman.

Then she says 'Goodnight,' and leaves.

She walks away unsteadily. Every so often she holds on to the sides of houses so as not to fall down. Then the houses come to an end, but all the same she crosses Libertador, heading towards the riverside. Wavering but on her own two feet, she reaches the wall. She thinks that at six o'clock in the morning, the colour of the river is somewhat depressing. They were laughing. Now Georgina can remember it distinctly. She looks down, almost tenderly. Tomorrow they'll read about it in the papers. It's so easy: all you need is a little push and then allow the body to fall all on its own, through its own weight. Splash. The word comes unbidden to her head, like a small explosion. She brushes the hair away from her face. Santiago had joined his palms over his breast and was clowning around. Georgina leans over the wall and vomits into the river. Now she feels better. The important thing is to live.

In front of her, the sky is turning red. She reckons that in just a few minutes the sun will come out. It's going to be a beautiful morning.

In the beginning (but not in the beginning of the beginning) a horse is going up in the lift. I know he is brown, but what I don't know is how he got there or what he is going to do when the lift comes to a stop. As far as that is concerned, the horse is quite different from the lion. And not only because the lion climbs the stairs in a reasonable manner, but also because, above all, the appearance of the lion has a logical explanation. I say to myself: there are lions in Africa. I say to myself: lions walk. I ask myself: if they walk, why don't they ever leave Africa? I answer myself: because lions don't have a particular destination in mind; sometimes they walk this way and sometimes that, and therefore, just going and coming, they never leave Africa. But that deduction doesn't deceive me of course. Even if they don't have a particular destination, at least one of the lions, unintentionally, might walk always in the same direction. He might walk by day, sleep by night, and in the morning, not aware of what he's doing, he might walk again in the same direction, then sleep again by night, and in the morning, not aware of what he's doing . . . I say to myself: Africa ends somewhere, and a lion walking always in the same direction will one day walk straight out of Africa and into another country. I say to myself: Argentina is another country, therefore that lion might come to Argentina. If he came at night, no one would see him because at night there are no people out in the street. He would climb the stairs up to my apartment, break the door without making a sound (lions break doors without making a sound because their skin is so thick and smooth), cross the hallway and sit down behind the dining room table.

I'm in bed; I know he is there, waiting; my blood throbs inside my head. It's very unsettling to know that there is a lion in the dining room and that he hasn't stirred. I get up. I leave my room and cross the dining room: on this side of the table, not on the lion's side. Before going into the kitchen I stop for a moment, turning my back on him. The lion doesn't jump on me, but that doesn't mean anything; he might jump when I come back. I go into the kitchen and drink a glass of water. I come out again, without stopping. This time the lion doesn't jump either, but that doesn't mean anything. I go to bed and wait warily. The lion isn't moving, but I know he's also waiting. I get up and go again into the kitchen. It is almost morning. On my way back, I glance sideways at the door. It hasn't been broken. But therein lies the real danger. The lion is still on his way; he will arrive tonight. As long as he isn't here, one lion will be like a thousand lions waiting for me, night after night, behind the dining room table.

In spite of all this, the lion isn't as bad as the horse. I know all about the lion: how he came, what he is thinking every time I go for a drink of water; I know that he knows why he doesn't jump every time he doesn't jump, that one night, when I decide to meet him face to face, all I'll have to do is walk into the dining room on that other side of the table. About the horse, on the other hand, I know nothing. He also arrives at night, but I don't understand why he has gone into the lift, nor how he manages to operate the sliding doors, nor how he presses the buttons. The horse has no history: all he does is go up in the lift. He counts the floors: first, second, third, fourth. The lift stops. My heart freezes as I wait. I know the end will be horrible, but I don't know *how* it will happen. And this is the beginning. Horror of the unexplainable, or the cult of Descartes, is the beginning.

■

But it's not the beginning of the beginning. It is the end of the beginning. The time has come when the little people inside the radio are soon to die, and God will also die, sitting cross-legged on top of the Heavens with his long mane and a gaucho's poncho. Because throughout the whole beginning, the world was made so that God and the dead could sit and walk *on top* of the Heavens; that is to say, the Universe is a hollow sphere cut by a horizontal plane; moving on that plane are we, the living, and this is called the Earth. From the Earth, looking upwards, you can see the inner surface of the upper hemisphere, and that is called the Heavens. Or the floor of the Heavens as seen from below. If you go through it, you can see the real floor of the Heavens, Heaven itself, on which the good dead walk and where God is sitting; to us, this seems difficult, because the floor of the Heavens is rounded, but the dead can hold themselves upright on a Heaven like that, and so can God, because He's God. Underneath our floor, inside the lower hemisphere, is the burning Hell, where little red devils float around together with the evil dead.

Now, before the end of the spherical universe, and before the lions and the horse, in the very heart of the beginning, are four cups of chocolate on a yellow plastic tablecloth. I'm four years old, and it's my birthday. But there are no guests, no cake with candles on it, no presents. The three of them are there, of course, sitting around the table; but in the beginning they don't count, because the three of them have always been there, and a birthday hasn't. I am alone in front of four cups of chocolate and a yellow plastic tablecloth. I'm moved to tears. This must be what it's like to be poor, and I'm supposed to feel terribly sad. The roof of the kitchen is made out of straw and the walls are of mud and my body is covered in rags; wind and snow seep through the cracks of my poor hut. I'm dying of cold and hunger while, in the palace, the spoilt little princess celebrates her fourth birthday with a ball: coaches at the door, dolls with real hair and a monkey that dances for the princess alone. I drink my chocolate. I weep inside my cup. And this really is the beginning. The trick of stories—the trick of the power of the imagination—lies in the beginning.

■

But this isn't the beginning of the beginning either. It is an awareness of the beginning. It is the beginning of an awareness of the beginning. Beyond this awareness, rising from behind strange faces like flashing images are a straw chair on a tiled courtyard, a wrinkled great-grandmother with a black scarf around her head, a madman climbing into a streetcar with a stick and, in the true beginning, a white hood. The white hood is mine. Or it was mine, I don't know, I don't understand what's happening, she has it on her head now. She arrived this morning and ever since she arrived everyone is fawning over her. I've been told she's my little cousin, but she doesn't look like my cousins because she isn't bigger than I am. She doesn't call me her baby, and she doesn't lift me up in her arms. But they lift her up in their arms, all the time, because she hasn't yet learnt how to walk, like the little babies in the park. I hate her. It's night-time already. They say she's going to leave, and they say it's cold out there. I run through the rooms. I throw myself against the legs of the grownups. I roll around on a mattress. I don't care if they scream at me, I'm happy; she's leaving. I look at her and it's there. She has my hood on. They say it looks big on her; they say she looks like a little old lady; they laugh. I'll sink her eyes in, like with a doll; I'll bite her nose off; I'll tear my hood away from her. Then it happens. Someone looks at me and says: 'Won't you lend your little cousin your hood?' I don't know what 'lend' means; I know I want to tear her up into small bits. I look at them. All eyes are fixed on me. Then I understand: all I need is a gesture, one single gesture, and the kingdom will be mine once again. They are waiting. They are laughing. I smile at them.

'Yes,' I say.

They laugh louder. They pinch my cheek and tell me I'm a darling. I've won. It's the beginning.

Further back, there is nothing. I look carefully for a taste of clementine, for my father's voice, for a smell of lip ointment. Something clean that will change my beginning. I want a white-washed beginning for my story. It is useless. Further back, there is nothing. That hood, my first infamy, is for ever the beginning of the beginning.

THE MUSIC OF SUNDAYS

To Gonzalo Imas

There was a moment in the afternoon—usually around four o'clock, perhaps five o'clock in the summer—when the old man would lean against the window, his head a little to one side, his hand pressed against the other ear, and say in a mournful voice: 'what a shame about the music.' By then we might have been talking for hours about the tangos of Magaldi or Charlo and all to please him because (as Aunt Lucrecia once said) there's no point coming to see him with a face like a wet weekend—we can make a little sacrifice to see him happy. In fact this little sacrifice was bigger than it seemed because if he was to enjoy his football as God intended (in his words), apparently the old man needed to feel a crowd around him. That meant we all had to stay glued to our seats until midnight because, as he put it, he wasn't going to sit down and watch even the league table with the other residents in the Home, they were a bunch of old farts, and once a Basque had got so excited about a Chilean goal that he took a great leap backwards, fell on his neck, and now he's pushing up daisies. So on Sunday nights we settled down in front of the television—Mom, Dad and me, Aunt Lucrecia, Uncle Antonito and even the twins—all grouped around the old man, who sported a knotted handkerchief on his head for the occasion and, in the absence of *chuenga*, that home-made gum you could buy at 1940s football matches, worked his jaws on a piece of old tire. It was even worse when Boca was playing: then it was the blue and gold shirt he stuffed in his mouth and not even Uncle Antonito, who's a devoted follower of River, dared crack a joke; the one time he ventured that somebody's goal had been offside, the old man jumped on him with such ferocity that if the twins hadn't stepped in — the old man dotes on them, never mind that they wear little hooped earrings and hair down to the waist — Uncle Antonito might have gone to join that codger who cheered the Chilean goal.

In short, other than an inadequate musical accompaniment, the old man really had nothing to complain about. So whenever he started harping on this theme about the music all we did was tell each other he had a screw loose and think no more of it. Until one afternoon Uncle Antonito, who was sick of hearing about the tangos of Corsini — and especially sick of the old man greeting him with the chant *You should see our goalie. What a star!* — which is how Boca fans celebrated their legendary goalkeeper in the 1920s — lost his patience and as soon as he heard 'what a shame about the music' he said 'What is this music you keep bleating about, Dad? Because the only music I ever hear is you yattering on all the blessed day.' But the old man stopped him there; he raised his hand in a signal to be quiet and said loftily: 'I'm not talking about the music I hear, Antonito, I'm talking about the music that's missing.'

I think if it had been left to the rest of us, the story would have ended there and then. I, for one, confess that I had absolutely no interest in ascertaining what glorious music it was that the old man found lacking in his life. I was beginning to tire of his whims;

it isn't exactly fun for a girl of my age to sit with her grandfather until midnight, screaming like a banshee every time someone scores a goal and all for the sake of making him feel loved. Uncle Antonito put it bluntly: If his problem is that he can't find some music or other, let him go and look for it up his sister's fanny. But the twins aren't the sort to give up so easily. They kept badgering the old man until finally he said: Well what music do you think I mean, boys? The music of Sundays.

Later they told me how they had coaxed out of him what he meant by the music of Sundays, something that had once been everywhere — or so he told them — and that you would have heard as soon as you woke up. They said he compared it to a communion or a symphony that ended only when night fell and the last of the lorries returned. Which lorries? I asked the twins. But I could scarcely make out their explanation with both of them laughing so much as they tried to imitate lorries making music.

The following week they came up with an idea: for the old man's birthday, their gift would be the music of Sundays. All the people in their building had already agreed to help: all we had to do was persuade my grandfather that this year the celebration was going to be at the twins' house (they live in a kind of tenement block, in Paternal) and bring the food; they would arrange everything else.

We protested, of course, but it's hopeless with the twins.

■

So on the Sunday of the birthday party there we were with our platters: Mom, Aunt Lucrecia, Uncle Antonito and me, waiting for Dad to arrive with the old man. The twins had instructed Dad to bring him as late as possible, and Dad agreed, but that turned out not to be such a good idea: the old man arrived in a foul mood and didn't say hello to anyone, merely observing that even the old neighbourhoods were a disgrace these days. He said that there was no communion any more, no harmony, and that nowadays everyone was looking out for themselves. It wasn't a promising start and things went downhill from there. I spent lunch wondering why I was wasting my whole Sunday in this tenement for the sake of pleasing some miserable old fantasist. By the time coffee arrived I had made myself a firm promise that this would be the last Sunday I sacrificed for the old man (and in fact it was). Perhaps we were all thinking the same thing, because suddenly we all fell silent, as though by design. And in the midst of our silence the sound of a radio came from the window. It was transmitting, rather louder than you'd usually expect, something that sounded to me like the Avellaneda Derby. See, Grandad, we were right, said one of the twins; you can still hear music in the barrios. The simulation had begun.

We looked at each other with resignation, because we already knew from the twins what was coming: lots of radios, turned right up, broadcasting different games from behind the windows, two or three lads in a doorway singing that chant the old man loves, a bunch of kids audibly kicking a ball around somewhere. And us, like a bunch of idiots, humouring him. That's not music, he said; you think one swallow makes a summer? Well I felt like chucking it all in and leaving then, but the twins were undeterred, insisting that no, the music of Sundays had not disappeared, that in the barrios you could still hear it in any street. And then with apparent spontaneity, they suggested we all go for a stroll to see if they were right. Showtime, Mom whispered to me, and Uncle Antonito snorted angrily.

We filed outside in a kind of procession. The twins went at the head; behind them was Dad, trying to soothe Uncle Antonito; then came Aunt Lucrecia with my grandfather. As we were leaving, Mom grabbed my arm and said: Wait, let's stay back a bit because this is the most ridiculous charade I've ever seen. So we went last of all.

We were walking very slowly, following the twins, and straightaway we began to hear radios. One or two in front of us, another, at full volume behind us, others, still faint, further off. From behind a thick wall, the voices of children could be heard; they were saying pass to me, they were saying come on, ball hog. Three boys sitting in a doorway started singing, just as we passed them, *You should see our goalie / What a Star! / He can stop a penalty / Sitting on a chair / If the chair breaks / We give him chocolate / Come on Boca Juniors / Down with River Plate!* I stole a sideways glance at the old man; for the first time that afternoon he appeared to be smiling. Cheers came from one house; their echo seemed to expand in the street. On the other side of the wall, the boys' shouting grew louder and more passionate as though this were no longer a performance but something on which their lives depended. The afternoon quietened, the noise of buses and cars fading away, while the voices on the radio got louder and more numerous, they were saying Negro Palma intercepts, they were saying Francéscoli moves forward, they were saying header from Gorosito, Márcico's waiting for the pass. I heard, or thought I heard, Rattin's name, but it couldn't be—wasn't he the one the old man said insulted the Queen back in the 1960s? I heard Moreno takes it on the chest, kills it with his left foot, turns and . . . Goooal! shouted the boys in the doorway, goooal! from the windows on that block, and from a different building too, and another further away. And some element of that shout lingered, as though caught in the air, I saw it in Dad's face, and in Aunt Lucrecia's; even Uncle Antonito seemed to sense it, something like a net being woven around us, gathering everyone together in the benevolent Sunday afternoon. Mom squeezed my arm, the twins looked at each other with amazement, the old man shook his head as though to say that it was true after all, the music was there, the music was still there. The doorway boys roared, the people in flats started arguing from one balcony to another. Mamita, mamita, shouted a boy coming towards us, and a startled mother looked up from the kitchen sink, elegant dodges were celebrated on vacant lots and patches of grass, Oléee-olé-olé-olá, they chorused in the stands, Look at us now, look at us now, they shouted in the streets, Come on Argentina / we won't stop cheering you, they sang in the halls, the roof terraces, the courtyards. And from far away came an unsteady noise, a murmur that kept growing louder, emanating from the very edge of the afternoon, that hour when people start listening to old dance songs and mulling, with contentment or bitterness, over the events of the Sunday that is ending. We saw them approaching, ever clearer in the hazy light of dusk, blowing their horns in time, a surging crowd of people waving blue and white flags, blue and red flags, red and white flags, gold and blue flags. Everybody in the neighbourhood came out to welcome them to the party, and the whole city rang with noise, like one unanimous, jubilant heart.

Afterwards would come the melancholy of Mondays, and there would be stories of fear and death, and later we would close the old man's eyes for the last time. But we would always know that under the sky of a distant Sunday, there had once been a music that had made us briefly happy and peaceful.

A QUESTION OF DELICACY

Señora Brun had almost finished getting ready to visit her friend Silvina when she noticed a little water coming from the spout in the bidet. She tried firmly closing the taps, but that didn't help. Then she opened them fully so as to close them again with more force, but no matter how hard she tightened them, hot water kept jetting out, now with enough pressure almost to reach the rim. She tried opening and closing the hot water tap again, to no avail: the flow was undiminished. Now the floor was wet and the bathroom full of steam and she herself was soaked so that there was no option but to turn off the hot water at the stopcock, change her clothes, and set about finding a plumber.

Not easy. The one who usually came to her house had jobs lined up for the next three days; the one the Neighbours' Association used couldn't come until the following afternoon. Finally, a plumber whose number was given her by the doorman in the building next along said he could be there in half an hour.

Señora Brun went downstairs to ask the doorman if the plumber was trustworthy.

'I don't know him, Señora,' said the porter. 'But these days you can't even trust your own mother.'

That was hardly reassuring but what choice did she have? She rang her friend Silvina and explained the setback.

'It's probably nothing and I can come later on,' she said.

As a precaution, she locked away her wallet and jewellery; she also rang her husband to tell him about the incident and to let him know that an unknown plumber was about to come to the house. Her husband would know what to do if anything untoward should happen.

The plumber, a wiry man in his fifties, arrived half an hour later, as promised. To Señora Brun's consternation, he wasn't alone, but accompanied by a large youth with long curly hair gathered in a pony-tail.

'Oh I didn't realise you would need to bring an assistant,' she said, very pleasantly. 'It's such a simple little job . . .'

'We haven't seen it yet, Señora,' the plumber said curtly.

He seems rather short-fused, Señora Brun thought. She led both the men to the bathroom and explained the problem.

'Where's the stopcock?' asked the plumber.

'Do you need to open it?' The plumber's expression was withering. 'Of course, of course, bear with me,' she said quickly, 'I'll go and do it.'

She went to the kitchen and opened the stopcock. Water started gushing out again. The assistant was turning something with a kind of spanner while the plumber gave him instructions.

'Oh dear, the whole bathroom's getting wet,' Señora Brun said.

'It's water, Señora,' said the plumber. 'It will dry.'

She sighed.

'Do you think that . . . ?'

'Now we need to turn off the stopcock,' said the plumber.

She ran to the kitchen, turned it off and came back.

'I'll need a cloth,' said the plumber.

She went to look for a cloth. When she came back with it the plumber was working. 'Dry this up a bit,' he said to the assistant. To Señora Brun he said, 'It's the washer in the hot water tap, but the transfer valve is broken, too. Did you know that it was broken?'

'No,' she said. 'It's always worked perfectly.'

'Perfectly?' said the plumber. 'Could you switch from the central spout to the side jets?'

'No, not really.'

'So it wasn't working perfectly. It's the transfer valve.'

'And will it take long to fix?'

'About half an hour. But I am going to need to turn the stopcock on and off a few times. It's probably better if you tell me where it is.'

The plumber's brusque manner made her uncomfortable but she decided that it would be better not to put up any opposition. You never know, with these people, she thought that she would say to Silvina when she recounted the incident later on, and she led him to the kitchen. She waited. The plumber opened the stopcock, shouted something to his assistant, who shouted a reply, then closed it again.

'Shall I go with you to the bathroom?' asked Señora Brun.

The plumber looked coldly at her.

'I think I know the way,' he said.

She waited for him to walk away then went to the study from where she could at least see the bathroom door. She felt like ringing her friend Silvina to tell her how unpleasant the plumber was but finally decided that it would be better not to call: with the door open the men were sure to overhear her and if she closed it she wouldn't be able to keep an eye on the bathroom door. One doesn't want to be on top of them, she pictured herself saying to Silvina; I don't like to keep monitoring people as they go about their work, but this plumber is such an odd character, and bringing that assistant, too—tell me, did the man really need to bring an assistant? You should have seen how he insisted on being the one to control the stopcock—what was I supposed to say? So now I've got him here, wandering around my house as if he owned the place.

She went to the bathroom.

'How's it going?' she asked cheerfully.

'Well,' said the plumber. 'It's nearly done.'

'Oh, thank goodness. I'll have time to visit my friend, then. She's laid up with a sprained ankle, poor thing.'

Neither the plumber nor his assistant had anything to say about that, so Señora Brun waited a little before deciding to go to her bedroom to get her clothes ready: she was going to change as soon as the plumber left so that she could go straightaway to her friend Silvina's house. She took the earrings she was going to wear out of her jewellery box and it was at that moment that she remembered the chain with the teardrop pendant: she had left it in the bathroom cabinet as she always did before getting into the shower. She tried not to panic: there was no reason why the plumber would open the cabinet.

She went to the bathroom and paused in the doorway, not wanting to appear anxious.

'So, everything all right?' she asked. 'You're nearly finished?'

'That's right, Señora,' said the plumber.

'And is it home for a rest after this?'

'Not yet,' said the assistant.

'What a difficult job,' said Señora Brun, 'always some last-minute emergency. Could you excuse me a moment? I need to get something.'

She stepped into the bathroom and opened the cabinet. A shiver of fear ran through her body: the teardrop wasn't there. Helplessly she glanced around her to see if it had been left on the vanity top or on a shelf or sill. Nothing. On the floor? Nothing.

'Oh no,' she cried involuntarily.

The plumber looked at her.

'Is something wrong?' he asked.

'No nothing, I just suddenly remembered something,' she said, and went out of the bathroom.

Of course I am sure, she imagined herself telling her friend Silvina, I always put it there before I have a shower (but just in case, she was checking her jewellery box, the chest of drawers, the bedside table). I make a point of putting it into the cabinet so that it can't fall down the drain—imagine how awful that would be, a three-carat diamond. No of course I don't wear it every day, do you think I'm mad, with all the insecurity there is these days? I keep it for special occasions and only if I'm going out with Ricardo. That's precisely the reason I wear it at home, where there are no risks. Otherwise when would I ever wear it? And I adore that teardrop.

She had looked in every conceivable place without finding it. What should she do now? Obviously I can't march up to him and say 'you stole my teardrop,' she imagined herself saying to Silvina. It's a question of delicacy, you know, one can't simply accuse someone of being a thief, without any proof. Besides, his character is quite . . . What if he sees red and thumps me on the head? Things could turn really nasty. And there are two of them; I'm lying there unconscious and in five minutes they clean out the house and no one will be any the wiser.

Señora Brun was standing in the middle of the hall, wondering how she ought to proceed; generally she favoured a delicate approach, but she couldn't allow the plumber to walk off with her diamond just like that. Most likely the man wasn't actually a professional burglar: he had spotted it in the cabinet, realised that it was valuable and pocketed it there and then. At that moment Señora Brun began to see a clear course of action: she must give the man an opportunity to return it. She let out a scream. The plumber had suddenly appeared before her eyes.

'Where are you going!' she shouted at him.

The man stared at her with surprise.

'To open the stopcock,' he said.

'Ah yes, of course, I'm sorry: my mind was somewhere else,' said Señora Brun.

She walked towards the bathroom thinking over what she was going to say. The boy with the curly hair was fiddling with the diverter tap.

'Turn it on,' she heard the plumber shout from the kitchen.

The boy turned the hot water tap. Water flowed out in a respectable stream. He turned the diverter tap: water came up from underneath. He turned it off: the flow of water stopped.

'Isn't that wonderful,' said Señora Brun. She pretended to be looking for something on the vanity top.

'Everything in order?' asked the plumber, who had just come into the bathroom.

'Yes,' said the boy.

'Oh my God!' cried Señora Brun. The plumber and the boy both looked at her. 'I could swear I left it right here,' she said, in an anguished tone; she waited for them to ask her to elaborate, but no. 'I'm so absent-minded, it's terrible. I don't suppose either of you has seen a little pendant on the countertop?'

Both of the men said that they had not.

'Oh, I could shoot myself! It has enormous sentimental value for me. My husband gave it to me when we got married. It had been his mother's, poor thing, she died so young.'

'Could you have left it somewhere else, Señora?' asked the plumber, a little impatiently.

'No, I'm sure I didn't.'

'Well, you can have a good look for it in a moment,' said the plumber. 'We're finished here.'

The man's got no shame, Señora Brun imagined telling her friend Silvina, but she had already thought this all out; the important thing was to give them an opportunity to return the necklace.

'Tell me,' she said, 'it couldn't have fallen down the plug in the basin, could it?'

'If you're asking can it, then yes it could,' he said. 'It all depends on the size.'

'It was very small,' Señora Brun said quickly. After all, if the man had it in his possession he was hardly going to say 'no, Señora, I happen to know that it's enormous.'

'Well then it could,' said the plumber.

'Would you be so kind as to have a look? I can make you both a coffee in the meantime.'

The plumber exchanged a glance with his assistant that did not escape Señora Brun's eye.

'Something cold will do fine, Señora,' said the plumber.

She went off to the kitchen. It was a shrewd move on her part to leave them alone, she felt. The thing was to give them time. If they weren't professional thieves maybe they would feel remorseful and when she returned with the drinks would say, Here it is; it was in the drain.

'And?' she said, returning with the drinks.

The man had taken the little grille out of the plughole in the basin.

'I can't see anything there,' he said.

'But what a disaster!' said Señora Brun. 'Please tell me it hasn't completely disappeared.'

The plumber looked at her with open hostility.

'No Señora,' he said. 'Nothing can disappear completely in this world.'

'So it must be somewhere,' said Señora Brun.

'Evidently,' said the plumber; he looked at his watch.

'Where?' asked Señora Brun. 'Where do you think it could be?'

'Well if it was washed down the drain it could be in the trap.'

'Oh, and couldn't you have a look there?'

'Look where?' asked the plumber.

'In the trap.'

The plumber heaved a sigh.

'It can be done, Señora. But it means removing the whole basin unit.'

'Never mind,' said Señora Brun. 'You can't imagine how important that little necklace is to me. I would be so grateful.'

'Señora, let's get this straight: you don't have to be grateful to me. I'll do what you ask and then I'll charge you for it. It's my job.'

'Of course, of course it's your job. That goes without saying. I'll keep out of your way. Take out everything that you need to. It'll probably turn up when you're least expecting it. I'll be close by. If you need me, give me a shout.'

And what else could I do, she imagined herself telling her friend Silvina, once things had got to that point—I had to give them one last chance, didn't I? Besides, the man looked like he wanted to wring my neck . . . One never knows how these people are going to react.

She paced anxiously between the study and the living room, listening to the banging. She was dying to go into the bathroom, but no: she had to give them time to talk about it together, to reconsider: she had read somewhere that even the worst criminals are capable of some feeling.

When the noise of banging had stopped, she went into the bathroom: her beautiful vanity counter with its marble top was on the floor and there were holes in the tiles.

Señora Brun pressed her palms together, as though in prayer.

'Please tell me you found it,' she said.

'Unfortunately not, Señora,' said the plumber.

She was furious then; this was going beyond a joke, she thought.

'But that's impossible!' she said severely. 'I left it here, on this countertop! Look again, carefully—it must be somewhere!'

'Yes, certainly. It's got to be somewhere,' the plumber said calmly.

The man's perverse, Señora Brun thought that she would tell her friend Silvina; he obviously enjoys tormenting me, but I'm not giving in so easily.

'So, what would you suggest as a solution?' she said.

The plumber, now without the slightest dissemblance, fixed Señora Brun with a cold, cruel stare.

'We can rip up the bathroom until we reach the drain box, if you like, to see in which section of piping your little pendant finally appears.'

He wants to kill me, Señora Brun thought. He looked at me with the eyes of a murderer, she imagined herself telling her friend Silvina, and I realised that if I tried to cross him, he would kill me.

'Yes, rip it up, rip it up,' she said. 'If you can guarantee me that my pendant's going to turn up.'

'Yes, Señora, it's going to turn up,' said the plumber with a controlled savagery. 'Sooner or later everything turns up.'

Señora Brun looked at him fearfully.

'But what if you don't find it even then?' she asked in desperation.

The plumber fixed his eyes on her.

'If we get down to the drain box and still don't find it, do you know what we can do?' He paused. Kill you, Señora Brun thought the plumber would say. 'We can carry on ripping things up until we reach the river. Because, if it isn't here, it must be in the river, right? The important thing is to find your little pendant.'

'The river, yes you're right, the river,' said Señora Brun, drunk on her own terror. 'If it's not here it's bound to turn up in the river,' she was surreptitiously edging towards the door. 'Rip it up, please, go down as far as the river. But quietly, please, very quietly because I'm going to have a nap. Help yourselves to drinks. My husband will pay you when he gets back.'

As she closed her bedroom door the banging started. Señora Brun took a sleeping pill and stretched out on the bed. In the moment she lay down her head she remembered that she had hidden the diamond teardrop there, under the pillow, hurriedly because the plumber had rung the doorbell just as she was taking it out of the jewellery box. It was a fact that, if the teardrop was there, her husband would never understand the need to rip up the bathroom, so she got up, went out onto the balcony, and threw the pendant far enough away that it would never be found. She wondered whether she would tell her friend Silvina this.

The banging was getting louder and louder, so before lying down again, she put in earplugs. Now they could smash things up as much as they wanted. Until they reached the drain box, or until they reached the river, or until nothing remained, not one stone upon another, of the safe and comfortable world Señora Brun had enjoyed.

THE CRUELTY OF LIFE

To my mother, at last

I was at the police station, sitting between a monobrow and a big girl, dark-skinned, who was breast-feeding her baby, and I felt sticky and verging on terrified after a five-hour peregrination on the most stifling March afternoon in living memory, and I was wondering if that intimation of terror owed more to my mother's disappearance or to the fact of not knowing what I would find, if I ever did find her, when for no apparent reason, the lion appeared. It wasn't the first time that had happened to me, that some troubling incident popped into my head out of nowhere, there was that room with the dancing legs, for example, and me watching them from under a chair and then the boy who came headlong through them, a boy with curly hair they called Moishke Copetón. From my vantage point under the chair, I couldn't grasp the concept of parties (even today I can't be doing with the crush and the noise) and caught none of the words except those very strange ones: Moishke Copetón. Whenever I remember that sea of legs it's an unchanging image, and it was the same in Precinct No. 17 of the Federal Police as I waited my turn between the monobrow and the brunette, when the lion burst in. Mostly it's the lion I see but that afternoon, rather than seeing him only from the vantage point of my bed, as he crouched behind the dining room table, I happened to switch the focus towards my six-year-old self, lying in the bed, sensing the lion. That was when—another blow—I realised that I couldn't think of him any more.

■

It wasn't that I had forgotten the lion: I could still imagine him (there was ample time to verify this before the police officer called me) crouching behind the dining room table, waiting for the perfect moment to leap onto me, and I could also see myself, fighting off sleep with my eyes stretched wide—because I was more afraid that the lion would catch me unawares than I was of the attack itself—huddled in the dark until it became so unbearable to keep still that I had to get up (to provoke the lion, forcing him to attack once and for all). I could also recall the voice of my father, asking from the other bedroom where I was going, the first time with concern, the second a little exasperated and the third on the brink of eruption (I was careful never to get up more than three times; then, as now, I would rather be mauled by a lion than endure certain tribulations of family life), and the unintelligible murmur of my mother, calming him down or perhaps poking fun at me. My mother never had much faith in people (and still doesn't now, truth be told). I could re-create the desperation I felt as I listened to Lucía sleeping soundly, a mere two yards from my bed—as though the world were not imperilled—and even reproduce the nightly sequence of thoughts with which I persuaded myself that a lion could indeed be waiting to pounce on me from behind the dining room table. What I couldn't do was *know* the lion; it was another sensibility, different to mine, that had been frightened of it. I saw her now, fearing the lion in the same way that I saw the lion—but that was all, for I was no longer that child who lay awake in the silence, eyes wide open, straining to interpret signs. It was as if the thread that connected me to her had weakened or broken. Is that what it means to *grow up?* There in precinct No. 17 it seemed an inadequate term to describe the passage of my years. Growing up. The concept alarmed me. Was I, in that respect, not so different to my mother? I'm getting old now, Mariúshkale, she had said to me on her eighty-fifth birthday but with a certain ambiguity, as though to say 'we both know that isn't so: old age wasn't made for me, I am invulnerable, my daughters are invulnerable, everything I have brought into the world is perfect and therefore immune to fever, pimples, melancholia, failure and death.' So all that rigmarole, dashing from pillar to post—was it just to come here and discover I'm like her? Not in a million years, I thought with a violence that made me shudder. The monobrow glanced over at me disapprovingly and a friendly nudge from the breast-feeder informed me that it was my turn.

■

What are his distinguishing features, asked the officer, disregarding the fact that this missing person—as I had just informed him—was called Perla and was my mother. Female, I answered. Sniggers at my back (I guessed from the monobrow) alerted me to the mistake. I was just so tired. I had endured so many grillings in police stations and hospital emergency departments, had tripped up so many times on the slippery police patter that even if I were to give a less vague answer than 'female' or 'white skin' I doubted it would spark any understanding in the face of my questioner — of course, of course I knew what he was after, but what was I supposed to say: lying in bed with her throat slit, officer? Lost an eye? A drooling stuttering wreck? And anyway, a few minutes earlier I had discovered something with such disheartening consequences for my future that nobody had any business expecting rational answers from me. Features, not sex, said the officer. I could feel the monobrow's raspy breath on my neck: he didn't like time-wasters. I said nothing. Distinguishing features — characteristics, prompted the officer. I wanted to tell him that my mother was, from top to toe, a distinguishing characteristic. I suffered, officer, how I suffered as a child because I longed to have a mother like all the other mothers; a longing she must have inculcated herself with her songs. The mothers in them, when they weren't blindly abandoning their children, in which case they were called heartless — which is to say unmotherly, given that the heart is the quintessential maternal organ, as can be deduced from that poem (often recited by my mother) in which the son, at the request of his cruel lover, stole his mother's heart as she slept (probably dreaming of him), and as he reached the dark threshold of his lover's house he stumbled and the heart called out 'Are you hurt, my son?' — when they had a heart, as I was saying, they were saints who prayed alone for the nation to bestow five medals on their five heroes or selfless old ladies washing clothes in the kitchen sink, welcoming home with open arms the disoriented son who had been seduced by some other world and swept by the dangerous new passions vice had taught him into a deep, churning sea. Mother! the delirious boy would cry on his return, I've been consumed by sorrow, bereft without your love. And she goes: Come here, scallywag, a kiss will make it better. That was how mothers were, according to the songs my mother sang. But not her. She neither cruelly abandoned me nor devoted herself to solitary prayer. And she did the washing, yes, but grumbling all the while, because she thought herself destined for something greater than the laundry. She must have had a heart, but it was arbitrary and deceitful. For instance, on the very day she first met El Rubio she had no option but to lie to him. How could she have had no option, I thought, lying in my parents' bed. It must have been a Sunday morning, because Sunday mornings in the marital bed were reserved for story-telling. The stories were always different. Sometimes they were nothing more than a detailed account of the previous evening's movie. (On Saturday nights Perla and El Rubio went to the cinema; he in a wide-brimmed hat and white silk scarf; she with a grosgrain rose pinned to her lapel and a hat that transformed her—Perla looked radiant beneath her hats as though these delicate creations of feathers, tulle or straw had the power to banish the little disappointments of her daily life.) That kind of story was told only once and presented no greater complexity than the plot of the movie itself, which was no small thing because Perla recounted every detail and even (as I found out in time) embellished a few so that, each Sunday as I pressed against the soft body that seemed to promise a safe harbour even as the voice filled me with fear, I would hear about one man's heinous scheme to convince his wife that she was going mad, or the dead woman in league with a housekeeper to torment her widower's new, young wife, or the deaf-blind girl savagely raped by a brutal man. What is 'raped,' I asked, intuiting some menace behind the word. It's the worst thing that can happen to a woman, said Perla, firmly, creating one of those pockets of darkness that I would struggle to elucidate on my journey towards the uncomfortable adulthood I occupied now, as I sat dumbstruck before the officer of Precinct No. 17, trying not to ask myself at which moment the thread had weakened or broken, if there ever had been anything like a thread, anyway. The films in themselves weren't necessarily disturbing because they always had a beginning and an end and no ramifications. The real-life stories, on the other hand, sometimes linked to stories from other Sundays, but they were unreliable links. And the story could get lost in the details. Or be nothing *but* details, as tended to happen with clothes. Clothes came as part of a story but then were described with so much theatre that they ended up becoming the story itself, like that party dress in lemon-yellow crepe, covered from top to bottom in rolled-up feathers that Perla called *aigrettes*, a diamante nestling at the centre of every single one. I had to make an effort not to picture my mother as a bird-woman, gigantic and malign with the face of a sparrowhawk and a feathery body, an image that returned to trouble me at night, like all the others, and which I had seen once in a book; I let myself be swept along by the words — *aigrette*, lemon-yellow, diamante: words whose significance I didn't always know but which submerged me in a beautiful haze that had no need of illustration because what was sketched by the words was, for me, better than any picture. When it came to the clothes, however, the process was complicated, not least because it meant believing Perla (how can a dress covered in feathers not be monstrous? Is it possible to distinguish a diamante in the centre of a rolled feather? Early on I suspected that Perla was exaggerating or changing things as she saw fit) but because it also forced on me the appreciation of a beauty that was alien to me. A holm oak, a pitcher, a wagon, these things appealed to my own notion of beauty, but lemon-yellow crepe transported me to a world I could only covet through Perla's own covetousness.

It was even worse with the accessories, which conferred on an outfit its crowning splendour. Perla, who had carefully drawn a design and saved her pennies to pay for the fabric and the making up and followed with a critical eye the work of the local seamstress until the dress of her dreams was finally a reality, had also given careful thought to the accessories. If even one was missing she would rather shut herself away in the house and never show off her new dress. And given that most of them were generally missing and she never had enough money to buy them she had to spend a long time working on the consciences of her five sisters (who were almost as selfish and quarrelsome as she was) until each one lent her what she needed. Only then, when everything was in its place, the grey beret picking up the collar of the little suit, the crocodile clutch bag in exactly the same colour as the shoes, the gloves no shorter or longer than they should be, would she puff up like a peacock and go wherever she had been invited. *I was so beautiful* (she would say, finishing her story in bed) *that when I came in everyone said I looked like a girl from the aristocracy.*

I didn't have a very clear idea of what the aristocracy was, but I knew that it was a state highly fancied by my mother. What confused me was that, in her songs, aristocrats were dreadful people who invariably thwarted the desires of Perla's heroes and heroines (consumptive worker-girls, dying orphans and starving poets). Hearing about these tragic lives, to which Perla gave somewhat cheerful expression, singing in the style of a chanteuse as she cleaned the house, I often wept for the world's wretches. But whenever we went out, all of us, even El Rubio, had to look like members of the aristocracy.

And speaking of El Rubio, why did you have no choice but to lie to him? I asked her eventually, because I was shocked that a girl would think of deceiving the man of her life on the very day she met him. Well it's simple, said Perla, like someone who's about to explain the most natural thing in the world: he had obviously asked me when my birthday was because he wanted to give me a present.

Perla had turned twenty-two only a month previously and telling the truth looked like wasting an opportunity. So she took two months off her life and he didn't disappoint her: on the afternoon of her fake birthday—they were already on their fourth or fifth date—he waited for her at the corner of Pringles and Guardia Vieja with a blue velvet box wrapped in tissue paper: inside, a little Girard-Perregaux watch.

It was that sort of attention to detail that made Perla fall so madly in love with him. Not only was El Rubio the kind of man to give a girl a beautiful bracelet watch, he also danced the tango vals better than anyone and in a café he would pay for everybody, as if he were loaded with money. His friends (Perla said) called him Paganini. One December afternoon, nearly a month after the fake birthday, he even turned up with a new DeSoto. But she didn't want to get in that day or indeed on their subsequent dates: it's frowned upon (she told him) for a single girl to get into the car of a single man. It was a shame because after the DeSoto he never had a car again in his life, and she loved cars. She used to imagine herself crossing Buenos Aires next to El Rubio in a gleaming *voiturette*. He never knew about that at the time. Patiently he would leave the DeSoto outside her house on Pringles Street, then the two of them would take a tram to Lezama Park: Perla adored going to Lezama Park—and singing tangos about dying lovers and having long conversations about her future. If he got sick of all that jacaranda and tuberculosis he didn't let on: he would never knowingly have slighted anyone. He did accidentally, though. One day during the carnival he arranged to meet Perla at the corner of Corrientes and Maipú and stood her up. Just like that, stranded amidst the streamers and the cheap cologne, in the ecru linen dress she had embroidered herself in cross-stitch.

And then she heard nothing more of him, apart from a photograph, sent months later from Ernesto Castro, *For Perla, From the beach*. No apologies, no promises, nothing to cling to. It should also be said that the photograph was dreadful: he was sitting on the ground near a kind of shack, in some get-up of shabby pyjamas, fraying hat and espadrilles, looking more like a vagrant than the tango-dancing object of her desire. (Sorting through other photos of El Rubio thirty years later—in Azul, in Olvarría, in General Acha—it struck me that his character was hard to pin down: he could just as easily be pictured as a bather or a gaucho; in an impeccable white suit and panama or in a T-shirt, swilling wine with low-lifers. The only thing we can know for sure is that he loved himself, I said to Lucía, and we couldn't stop laughing, despite the whispering presence of death. Because he was always taking photographs of himself: in good times and bad. And he even had the nerve to send Perla, who was all willowy elegance and cross-stitch embroidery, that one in which he looked so ugly in the scruffy hat.)

We'll never know how she came to reconcile the vagrant with the Paganini. She must have been broken-hearted because for five years she continuously sang that tango *Be gone! Don't come here begging me to remember each hour of our tragic romance.* But the fact is that she turned twenty-three, twenty-four, twenty-six, rejecting one after another, all the suitors who presented themselves to her.

At twenty-seven she went to see a gypsy. (My mother was an odd kind of Jew: she liked priests for their sermonising and gypsies for their fortune-telling, not to mention that every Good Friday she took us to the cinema to weep over the Passion and Death of Our Lord Jesus Christ.) The gypsy told her that she was going to meet the love of her life soon and give him her left hand. She foresaw a home in which there would be daughters but no money. The money won't stay, she said; it's going to come in and go out but never stay. Since she was desperate to be rich, Perla decided not to believe the gypsy's prophecy. And six days later she was waiting to meet a new suitor in the house of the only one of her sisters to have married a millionaire.

The thing she most liked about that house was the Baccarat crystal chandelier in the dining room and what she most disliked was the deep, bitter line on her brother-in-law's forehead and the wart beside his nose. Subconsciously she assigned the same line to the suitor who was at that moment making his way to the house. She was wrong. That man was a brick, affable and kind. En route to the house he ran into a friend who had just arrived from Bahía Blanca taking advantage of a free passage given to him by virtue of the Eucharistic Congress that was being held in Buenos Aires. There and then the brick invited his newly arrived friend to share in his good fortune.

'I've been invited round to someone's house,' he said. 'Apparently they're going to introduce me to a pretty girl. Do you want to come along?'

The friend did want to. It was El Rubio.

Of all that happened in that house the one salient fact is that Perla gave El Rubio her left hand to shake because the right one was bandaged up. Knowing her, it isn't too far-fetched to suppose that the bandage may have been somehow contrived, because she was always a cheat, which isn't to say that events didn't transpire exactly as she told them — that two days earlier she got a nasty burn on her hand and needed to bandage it — because it's also true that there was always something a bit magical about her.

At any rate, afterwards, when the two men were in the street, barely had his friend ventured a few words on how pretty Perla was (he called her Perla, without compunction) than El Rubio stopped him dead.

'Be careful what you say,' he said, 'because that woman is my fiancée.'

And he must have known what he was saying because eight months later they were married.

■

So when did you tell him the truth? I ask, in my parents' bed, more concerned about the moral problem than about the story itself. And not surprisingly. Why would any child familiar with that tale of the girl who plays next to a pond with a gold ball, accidentally drops it in, then gets in return a toad that finally turns out to be a prince, be much impressed by the story of a man who turns up after a five-year absence at the house of the brother-in-law of the woman who's been waiting for him? The very least one asks of any story is that there be an element of chance in the plot. The problem of truth, on the other hand, does worry me. Although not in the way it worries Lucía, who believes that one should always tell the truth, regardless of the circumstances, because it's the right thing to do. The problem of truth worries me because I can't imagine going through life with the weight of certain lies on your back. A fake birthday, for instance. There are literally millions of things relating to a person's birthday, so if you are going to lie to one person about your date of birth, in order for that lie never to be discovered, you're going to have to keep modifying each of those millions of things for the rest of your life, not only for the sake of the person to whom you lied but for all those others to whom the deceived person may speak at some time or other. The complications are infinite, beginning at the moment of the lie and ending only at death. All of which goes to show that lying did not actually constitute a moral problem for me. It was a purely practical question—even if, in front of Lucía, I was prepared to swear that the act of lying was abominable in itself. That was a lie that didn't frighten me because I considered it a matter of self-defence and because it replaced a hazy concept about good and evil that I felt impinged on me, although I wasn't able to explain it. Besides, it was a lie that began and ended with Lucía (it was cut to her size), which exempted me from having to apply it to millions of cases.

Perla, on the other hand, has no problem lying. Neither in the moral sphere nor in the practical one.

'I honestly can't remember at what point I told him the truth,' she says, putting an end to the question.

■

That's typical of my mother, managing to work herself into the story in a way that reflects well on her and gives her a greater role than the one originally allotted her: that of missing person. But whether she likes it or not, her presence here is incidental and the hunt for her through hospitals and police stations—plus an episode featuring the Happiness Care Home, still to come—is merely the backdrop to this story's real drama: the missing lion. I could have discovered its absence at any time, but it had to happen on the same day of the other loss, while Lucía was looking for my mother in one direction and I in another, communicating all the while via a complicated system of messages because, to make matters worse, the woman—or guardian angel—who usually helped my mother had gone off to La Plata on some urgent business that meant she couldn't serve as a bridge between us.

It was in the midst of this chaos that I realised I had lost the lion but, what if I had made the discovery on a quieter day? Would I have managed to avoid becoming the creature I was for the next two years (exactly until the morning in March when we visited the Happiness Care Home)? Drained, muddle-headed, incapable of any thought that didn't somehow rebound back on me and my obvious stupidity? I would reach for a tin of biscuits and some awareness of the banality of that action would detain me halfway, crushed by a suggestion of failure. It didn't stop me from eating the biscuit after all, but even such a small event held no pleasure for me. It's an unpleasant sensation, especially for someone who has built her life on the supposition of a certain eccentricity or state of grace. Now I knew that that state, if it had ever existed, was deep in the rock bed of my past and not able to illuminate my present, and that the woman whose hand had reached for the biscuit tin didn't deserve a jot of sympathy from me.

It may seem extravagant to some that a missing lion had depressed me to this degree but the thing is that, of the three or four formative events that have seemed to shape my life (inconspicuous events which I have nevertheless loaded with significance and allowed to shed light on my every act, however trivial, oh there she is the oddball, reaching out to pinch a biscuit, how crudely her brain grapples with such a simple act, how clearly she sees herself, pathetic, greedy, looking for the one with the most filling; and then, somehow redeemed by my own pitiless gaze, I could calmly savour the biscuit like someone eating consecrated bread), of those three or four episodes, as I was saying, two actually feature lions. In the first of these I'm four or five years old. I'm running in

circles around my grandmother's patio while, in an effort to miti-
gate my disappointment in the real world, I invent a story of which
I am the heroine and in which people I don't like get their come-
uppance while other extraordinary people praise me for my charm
and courage. Each time some incident or character doesn't fit into
the picture I have to change it, thus imposing other modifications
which in their turn bring new imperfections that I have to remedy.
As I get closer (or so I think) to the perfect version of my story, my
excitement mounts and I spin around faster and faster. I'm now
at a vertiginous point, on the cusp of a time when all difficulties
will be over and I'll be happy. Then, behind me, coming from the
kitchen door, and with the same effect as something heavy falling
on my head, I hear: 'She looks like a caged lion.'

The second is not so much an episode as a line of thought,
one I follow night after night and which leads mercilessly to the
lion. I'm in bed, sensing his presence, and he is behind the dining
room table, waiting for the moment to leap on me. All my nights,
between the ages of five and eight, are marked by this awareness
of the lion. And what I had discovered in Precinct No. 17 of the
Federal Police was that the complete memory was there and that
I could recount it as often as I liked and pretend to be recounting
part of my life, but that for some time now—how long?—I had
been telling somebody else's story.

My actions had been emptied of meaning, something like
that. And my punishment was to know it. Perhaps one day my sto-
lidity would reach a point where I could not even recognise that
turn of events and I would go through life as a perfect imbecile.
For the moment I was a mutant, awaiting my transformation—

into someone else? into myself? I still didn't know from which point I was observing the phenomenon. Like a good mutant, I didn't have an assigned category.

On the bus or queueing up to pay taxes I surreptitiously studied my fellow men and women. I envied them deeply: they seemed to bear no shadow of worry. I tried a few experiments to speed up the process of transformation. One morning, at the Water Company, I nearly managed it. I was waiting in a crowded area to arrange payment of an outstanding debt which—or so I hoped—would turn me in more than one sense into a good citizen. People were talking all around me. Hearing themselves speak seemed not to bother them. Perhaps they didn't even hear it. They talked to fill the time and because it was easier to talk than to endure the silence. I decided to join in. First I agreed with a blonde lady that you come to pay your bill and they treat you worse than a criminal, then I made a few contributions to a plan one bald fellow had to get the country booming and vibrant in less than a year. This time no inner laughter distanced me from my companions. I was who I claimed to be, nothing more and they—you could tell a mile off—accepted me without question. I was just beginning to feel comfortable in my role when a voice from nowhere murmured: Art thou, indeed, that woman? Now I see that in a way these words anticipated what I would later discover at the Happiness Care Home. And not because of the question's meaning: it was typical of the recriminations that regularly interrupted my actions, leaving me speechless, that particular afternoon, in front of my fellow queuers, neither able to speak to them nor to call on the vanity that would have distanced me from them in times past.

Not, as I said because of the words' meaning, but because of that archaic style which reminded me of the question the Sleeping Beauty asks, at the moment she opens her eyes, after sleeping for a hundred years and sees the Prince, who has just woken her with a kiss on the lips. *Who art thou Sir, and what dost thou here?* a line to which I had returned time and again, trying in vain to penetrate its perfection and wondering if I, woken abruptly after my hundred-year sleep, could have formulated such a rigorous question, condensing—and so politely!—everything that needs to be known in such unwonted circumstances. That flashback should have alerted me, but I was so absorbed by my loss that I didn't even think about how old-fashioned—or bloody-minded—my subconscious can be left to its own devices. Not to mention Sleeping Beauty. I didn't let myself think of her, or of the girl spinning in the patio or of the lion. These thoughts felt plundered; they belonged to another person. That girl who *knows* the lion, with every fibre of her being and can sense him from her bed, not the woman crying for his loss.

Bed is the place for big problems. When Lucía's asleep, when Perla and El Rubio are sleeping, Mariana can mull over her big problems without anyone coming to scold her for not doing anything. Is thinking not doing anything? In fact that is one of the big problems she can devote herself to considering when nobody's around to bother her. When she's not in bed, the only other time she can devote herself to thought is when she's pretending to be a dog—and she only does that on cold days. On hot days Lucía's feet don't get freezing so she doesn't ask Mariana to come and sit on her like a dog. Lucía feels the cold easily, but not Mariana. She likes to feel an icy wind on her face and she loves frost. What she most likes about frost is the word frost. If she thinks: This morning when I went to school the street was covered in frost, she can believe that she's in one of those story-book countries where people use sledges to get around. When it's very cold, her mother says: Today it's a frosting cold, turning frost into a verb and calling to mind cake decoration, which isn't nearly as pretty. Her mother comes up with some strange verbs, sometimes. If she's eaten a lot she says: I'm stiffed. Mariana has never heard other people use either of these words and much less the word musgrevely. It's a word that features in a very sad song her mother sings that goes: Little Paper Boy they called him and he to see them all musgrevely. So Mariana reckons that musgrevely means demonstrating to others that you are what they think you are. They called him little paper boy and he, without deception, showed that he was one. She even has the impression that he was proud to be musgrevely. But sometimes it seems to her that the song says 'Little Paper Boy they called him he could see them all most easily.' Although the day they argue about it Lucía says that neither version is correct. What the song says, according to Lucía, is: Little Paper Boy they called him and he to sea had set out previously. In that case, he had been a sailor before he was a paper boy. The problem is the next bit, says Mariana, who always listens carefully to her mother's songs. What's the next bit? asks Lucía, who doesn't pay them much attention. Mariana sings: Little Paper Boy they called him and he could see them all most easily, when one day on a street corner a mother with no intestines abandoned him to fate. It's *entirely baseless* says Lucía, who has read William Saroyan. The two roll around laughing because thinking of that reminds them of the other preposterous lyrics their mother sings, that one about the suicidal lovers, says Lucía breathless with laughter and Mariana sings Goodbye mother, goodbye father, goodbye brothers and sisters, we must go now and we won't see each other again; if our love on earth was true, in the tomb it will be even greater. Every time they're about to stop laughing they remember some new example—that one that begins I loved her with the gentle soul of my evidence, says Lucía; *entirely baseless,* says Mariana—and they're off again. The trouble is that there are songs they have never heard anyone else sing and the only time they dare to ask their mother if the song about the paper boy is 'he could see them all most easily' or 'to sea he'd set out previously' she looks at them as though they were completely mad and says: haven't you two got anything better to talk about? She's like that, their mother, it's impossible to get the better of her. She always finds a way to turn things round and walk off cool as a cucumber. She says, 'I'm stiffed,' and she says musgrevely and nobody will ever know where she gets these words from. Like sarcirony. Their mother is always using the word sarcirony. She says: Don't look at me with sarcirony, and she says: He said it with sarcirony. Mariana understands perfectly what sarcirony means. She herself often speaks with sarcirony. And so does Lucía. And El Rubio. They're a very sarcironic family. But then one day she writes sarcirony in an essay and the teacher crosses it out with a red pencil and says that the word doesn't exist. She refutes this and even explains the significance. But the teacher makes her look it up in a dictionary and that's when Mariana discovers that her mother can never be entirely trusted, even when she's using a beautiful word like sarcirony.

Lucía, on the other hand, does know how all the words should be because she reads the dictionary. She takes it with her into the bathroom and spends hours locked in there where nobody can bother her. The dictionary is a bit battered and has a story that predates Mariana's birth. Stories from before her birth give her a hollow feeling in the heart. Not the ones from the time her mother and father first met, because those are so old they're practically fables. The ones about her mother and aunts when they were children even more so. There were six Malamud sisters (not counting the boys) and all of them were wild, but the wildest must have been her mother, because now they're all old ladies and she's still wild. Mariana loves the stories about the Malamud sisters because they were very poor and very prankish and laughed at everything, and because they lived next door to a family of cheerful and friendly Italians who ended up being Mafia chiefs. By contrast, the stories in which Lucía features but isn't yet born give her that sense of emptiness because they show that her mother, father and Lucía lived happily without her and had no need of her existence. She hates that—but nothing is as infuriating as the dead girl. The dead girl appears in some of these stories from the past. Lucía and her mother talk about this child and about how they waited for her and some of the things that happened while they were waiting, but they never mention the thing that causes her the most fear—and not any kind of fear but a peculiar, retrospective kind. They never say that she would not be in the world had this child not been born dead, and that nobody would be any the wiser. Mariana hates this child and is tremendously happy that she's good and dead. But that also frightens her, since the worst thing you can do in life is take pleasure in the death of another person, especially a sister, so she can't tell anyone about this and it's the most terrible secret she keeps. That dictionary dates from the time of the dead girl. It was given to Lucía before the child was born, because nobody knew that she would be born dead, so they were happy and brought round presents. Apparently it came on a little shelf, with six story books, three on either side of the dictionary. Mariana's never seen a mini-bookcase: she believes that it has been her lot to live in a time in which there aren't such beautiful objects. She enquires about the storybooks that came with the dictionary. Nobody knows anything, nobody remembers anything, they have disappeared without a trace; vainly she tries to imagine the splendour of those books which will never again be possible on earth. It's unfair that all that is left of such a splendid collection is the dictionary. She hates dictionaries and that whole business of the words being listed alphabetically. In fact she despises alphabetic order, the ABC strikes her as the most boring system in the world—there's no way to learn it because there's no reason in it. If something can't be rationalised, it can't be learnt. She used to think that the letters came in an order of familiarity so that you would simply need to decide which was the better known of two letters, the N and the R, for example, and that way work out the position of each letter, but—what was the K doing before the M? And the S after the Q? With the alphabet the only option is to learn it parrot-fashion and it's a shame to see the words arranged that way, with some very boring definition underneath them, it makes them ugly; she likes to see a word in the middle of other words so that, even if you've never heard it before in your life, you work out what it means and it's like a game. But Lucía loves the dictionary and spends hours locked in the bathroom reading it so as not to be disturbed. Or perhaps it just seems like hours to Mariana because she's on the other side of the door waiting for her sister to come out so that they can play together. When her sister's in the bathroom, Mariana imagines that if she comes out and they play she'll be happy, but when Lucía does emerge it's hard to believe that happiness can ever be attained: Lucía gets furious because, even though Mariana said—and repeated—that Lucía can stay in there forever, for all she cares, that she'll never ask her to come out, ultimately she hasn't been able to bear the wait and has ended up calling her, which (as she already guessed would happen) seems bound to have unhappy repercussions. Not on one occasion, though. That time her dream comes true because Lucía, after her confinement with the dictionary, comes out of the bathroom looking for her: she wants Mariana to listen to a song she composed in the bath about her yearning for an encyclopedia. Mariana knows what that is because, a few days ago, when her sister mentioned wanting one for the first time, she asked: Luci, what is an encyclopedia? And Lucía gazed into the distance and said: It's a book that has all knowledge in it. She had to make a great effort to imagine that totality of knowledge and another, even greater, to imagine a book big enough to contain it. Was this really the way things were? That Lucía locked herself away to read a dictionary but really wanted an encyclopedia? That she longed for her sister to come out of the bathroom only to regret it and feel even more wretched than before? That perfection was impossible in this world? At any rate, the afternoon that Lucía seeks her out to sing the song she composed in the bath comes pretty close to perfection.

The song tells of Lucía's longing for an encyclopedia, about the money that would be necessary to buy one, and ends abruptly: *And since I haven't got it I'll just have to wait.* Straight to the point, the way Lucía likes her poetry. *What is poetry? You're asking me? Poetry is you.* They say what they want to say, no messing around. But things are rarely so simple. That business with Amado Nervo, for instance—Mariana can't even bear to remember that ill-fated afternoon, with Lucía lying in bed reading Nervo's *The Immovable Beloved* and her being a dog, never happier. She doesn't even like the title of Nervo's book, imagining a paralysed woman in a wheelchair whom she can't imagine anyone loving, let alone writing poems for but, to be on the safe side, she's never told Lucía that. And then her sister says: Listen to this poem. Lucía always reads her things she really likes and Mariana loves it, especially when she reads her the funny bits out of novels, because she can understand them and they both roll around laughing. But this time she puts on that tone she uses when she's going to read something sublime so, with trepidation, Mariana prepares to hear the world's most beautiful poem. It's called *Cowardice*, her sister says, and that reassures her, because Mariana knows very well what cowardice is: it's the worst thing after treachery and no hero ever forgives it. But in the poem Lucía's reading nobody flees the battle or quakes in the presence of the enemy. The beloved woman walks past with her mother—whose presence in a love poem is already questionable—and has hair the colour of flaxen wheat. Mariana doesn't know what flaxen wheat is but can't help picturing the beloved wearing a kind of bush on her head. To make things worse, all the wounds the poet has on his body—we don't know how he came by them but there seem to be an awful lot—start opening up and bleeding in front of the beloved and the beloved's mother. The poet says very sadly that he let them walk past without calling out to them, but Mariana can't help feeling that this was for the best, since he's gushing blood. Things are no clearer by the end of the poem. Did you like it? Lucía asks. Yes, Luci, she says. Then Lucía, who has a mean streak, says: Explain it to me. It's the most awful moment of her life. She can only think of the wounds all opening up at once and the scene seems revolting to her but it's too late to say that. Is she a coward? Undoubtedly. Why did you say you like it if you didn't understand a single thing? Lucía says. She's unyielding and merciless, and when she's with her, Mariana doesn't know which is worse, to get things wrong about art or to tell a lie. It's not like with God, who can look into her head and so knows why she lies when she does and knows that she doesn't do it to hurt other people but rather to benefit herself—and God's fine with that. It's so reassuring to have someone really know how you are and not to have to keep giving explanations. Besides he's happy with her because she talks to him like a normal person, unlike the others who are always sucking up to him. God finds her approach to life refreshing. Every night, when the light goes off, she puts her hands together as she's seen people do in the illustrations of books, and she asks him for things she wants. She can't kneel beside the bed because Lucía would notice, but God doesn't mind about things like that. He knows perfectly well that she can't kneel because she's Jewish. She doesn't fully understand what it means to be Jewish, it's annoying that she can't take communion and that, at school, instead of studying Religion, which is so lovely with all those lives of the saints, she has to take Moral Philosophy which seems to be the opposite of Religion, though she doesn't entirely understand what it's about and neither, it seems to her, does the teacher. In one class she makes them write an extremely dull essay on thrift, in another she reads them *The Brave Little Tailor* and in another she recites a poem about a peach that must not be allowed to stain the immaculate whiteness of the dress belonging to the little girl eating it, because the stain will never come out. At the end there's something about wicked deeds but it's the least interesting part of the poem and Mariana can't help thinking that if the author wanted to talk about wicked deeds he should have put them up at the start. The only thing she learns from the poem is that, of all the things that may stain a dress, a peach is the worst and from then on, although her clothes are quite messy and often have ink marks or chocolate and other kinds of stain on them, every time she eats a peach she takes extra precautions because, thanks to that poem, she's convinced that if peach juice falls on her dress she may as well throw it out—the stain won't ever come out. But this doesn't help her to understand fully what it means to be Jewish. Her mother will say of a person who fasts on the Day of Atonement that he or she is 'very Jewish' as if that were rather admirable, but she makes no great effort herself to be very Jewish: on the Day of Atonement she simply eats little. Going without food makes me feel listless, her mother says, and she seems sure that that's an incontestable reason not to fast. Mind you, I don't eat very much, she says. Mariana thinks that her mother is not very Jewish and her father even less so than her mother, because he eats the same as usual on the Day of Atonement, and Lucía least of all because if she's told she has to go to the synagogue to see her grandparents on the Day of Atonement, she vomits and falls ill. Clearly as a family they are scarcely Jewish at all, but she still can't kneel beside her bed or say Little Jesus I Love Thee, because that's what the goy do. It's quite complicated: she can *not* do the things Jews do but can't *do* the things the goy do, so instead of saying Little Jesus I Love Thee, she says Little God I Love Thee. And she prays to him with her hands together every night, when nobody can see. As for asking, she does that one thing at a time because God may know what she's like, but he has no reason to know all the things she wants. There are things she wants just once and things she wants all the time: she asks God for those every night. One of the things she asks for every night is that, in six and a half years, when she's the same age as Lucía is now, she'll know as much as Lucía. And a little bit more. The trouble is that Lucía wants her to know everything now, because otherwise she's an idiot. Who wrote *The Iliad?* asks Lucía when they're playing Questions and Answers one day. Homer, she replies. Who wrote *Don Quixote of La Mancha?* Miguel de Cervantes, she says. Who wrote *The Divine Comedy?* Lucía asks. (Sometimes, when they aren't playing, Mariana likes to imagine that they are playing Questions and Answers and that Lucía asks her a question that is so difficult she never would have imagined such a young girl being able to answer it. And she answers brilliantly! But imagination doesn't get you far with Lucía. Who wrote *The Divine Comedy*, is what she asked.) Since Mariana hasn't the faintest idea who wrote *The Divine Comedy*, she can't even invent an answer to cover her ignorance. So she opts for the moral high ground. Valiant, honourable, true to the last, she lifts her gaze and says, I don't know, Lucía. But her sister, impervious to this moment of moral high standing, tells Mariana she's a moron anyway. You moron, she says, how can someone of six years old not know who wrote *The Divine Comedy*? And the game ends there.

'You're twisting everything!'

This is new. For Lucía to butt into the story is totally unexpected. And anyway, she isn't twisting anything. She's simply telling her version of the facts.

'That's not true. You're only telling a part of it, which isn't the same thing. And the part that makes me look like a monster, too. But, who used to play Shopkeeper with you? And who made you fairy bites? And, by the way, this doesn't count as butting in, it's self-defence.'

The Shopkeeper thing is undeniably true. In the afternoons when they sat at the table in the little kitchen to have their milk, Lucía used to be the Shopkeeper. How much cheese would you like, Señora? Would you prefer a baguette or a French loaf? Then brandishing the knife she would cut with the firm but generous hand of our local shopkeeper. Mariana loved it when Lucía pretended to be a shopkeeper. Every afternoon, watching Lucía prepare the milk, she waited for those minutes of happiness to arrive.

'You see? Your subconscious has given you away. *I* prepared the milk, *I* cut the cheese, *I* made the pancakes. You sat and watched.'

She sat and watched. And gave instructions. She knew it all, the *theory* of everything: how much flour the pancakes needed, what a bain marie is, how to stir the milk so that it doesn't stick.

'And what about the *torrejas?* Bet I've got you there.'

She had indeed. Mariana hadn't the slightest idea how to make *torrejas*. She knew as little on this subject as Lucía did, worse luck. Because sometimes they both had an unbearable urge to eat *torrejas*—the word alone sounded like a promise of happiness. They knew they had bread, and perhaps eggs and honey, but they didn't know how to make them. So they would spend a long time discussing the properties that something with such a beautiful name ought to have, throwing in everything crunchy, everything golden and delightful that is possible on earth. Perhaps it's for that reason (and also because of the way life's absurdities could make them laugh and laugh, clutching their sides and weeping helplessly) perhaps it's for that reason that over the years, and despite their differences—I pretended to be a dog to warm up your feet, and I had to make your hot milk, I had to look after you all the time because you were a bit stupid—despite the roles, never abandoned, of younger and older sister, they still turn to each other when all else fails.

But let's not get sentimental. These girls have a peculiar relationship—otherwise there's no pathos.

'You see, that's what I mean. You don't continue with the *tor-rejas* theme because all the perverse stories serve your purpose better. I wonder what else you've left out?'

The fairy bites, for sure. She promises to come back to the fairy bites, but not right now. She's losing the flow, her characters are rebelling and she, usually so careful—this event here, the other one further on, avoid sentimental outpourings unless they're relevant because if all the elements aren't in the right place there's no story—so I lock myself at home and don't come out until someone lends me a little grey hat? Shh—who's this interrupting now?—she's starting to realise that this story, which began with a fairly orthodox *I*—though perhaps it was teetering even then—and the discovery that she's lost the lion, has cunningly slid towards a *she*, who far from confronting her loss tiptoes around the edges, as though venturing that nothing serious has happened here, neither pimples, nor failure nor death. A phrase that can't help but lead back to my supposed similarity to Perla. And that's not the story. The story is the lion, how I lost it and how I sat petrified in front of the officer who was asking now for the third time: You can't recall any distinctive characteristics of the missing person?

None, I said; not one. And with a bovine docility I got the rest of the questions over quickly, so that the monobrow would have no cause for complaint and the nursing mother would think, how nice, what a normal mother this lady has, how normal and loving and perfect all the mothers of the world are and this lady too, even if she isn't a mother, poor thing, how normal she seems.

Conclusion: I left Precinct No. 17 as ignorant of my mother's whereabouts as I had entered it and with this new problem of not being able to think of the lion. Heat swept over me like an infernal wave.

I looked for a public telephone. From the answering machine in my house, Lucía's voice dazed and discouraged, outlined the steps she had taken, the ones she would take next and her readiness to die; on the answering machine in her house I recorded my own recent adventures and my own desire not to die without first killing all the old people in the world. I also rang my mother's house, just to be safe, although I knew that the Guardian Angel could not yet have returned from her business in La Plata. You go to La Plata, I had said to her less than six hours earlier. Lucía and I can manage. What rubbish, Lucía and I can't manage anything that isn't *The Divine Comedy* or *torrejas*. Or rather the illusory taste of *torrejas*, because we still haven't learnt how to make them. You concentrate on your studies, Perla used to say, when the time comes that you need to cook I'm sure you'll pick it up. Another of her lies: we know our way around a formula for deoxyribonucleic acid or a hendecasyllable but the simple prospect of frying an egg paralyses us. The Guardian Angel would certainly have been able to find Perla, she knows what to do in these situations, she is competent and friendly; at the very least she could have taken me into her lap, I've lost my little rooster taloo talay I would have sung, in the words of the nursery rhyme, and she would have wrapped me in her great angel wings and my mother and the lion and all the lost things screeching at that moment in my head would have vanished from the face of the earth. But she wasn't home, taloo talay. I hung up and walked aimlessly around Las Heras: all I wanted was to sit down in some doorway and sob my heart out. There, on my right, were the steps leading up to the Faculty of Engineering—why not stop there? After all, I didn't have Perla dogging my every step, making sure I didn't fall over, or bump into something, or cry, what reason have you got to cry, Mariúshkale, when I've given you everything, cod liver oil to make you the strongest, green apples to make you the most intelligent, stories to feed your imagination, little piqué dresses to make you look aristocratic. What more could you need, my darling daughter? The lion, mother, I need the lion and the sad thing is that I should have realised before, this very morning I could have thought of it, instead of staring like an imbecile at the computer screen, all my energy invested in online patience as if existence came down to this, putting a red Queen beneath the black King, a black Jack beneath the red Queen, moving to the right-hand box the Ace of Spades, the two of Spades, the three of Spades, as though the minute movement of the mouse that generated this displacement of cards on the screen were enough to keep me from noticing a fait accompli: that it wasn't through mere distraction or poetic idleness that I had been momentarily diverted from a path towards *greatness*. My God, how long had it been since I last spoke that word, and not with coy italics but loud and clear with the head-to-toe conviction that the girl who had invented a lion from her bed could aspire to nothing less. And yes. Perhaps she could. Except that (I could have found this out playing patience if the phone hadn't rung then) the diversion wasn't momentary and appeared to have no solution because I was no longer that girl.

The phone rang just as I was putting a red nine beneath a black ten. I rushed to answer. Was I expecting the call of the muse or of eternal youth? It was neither of these. In fact it was the Guardian Angel: Señora Ema has just called me. Your mother was supposed to be there at noon but she hasn't arrived. She left here at twenty to eleven and seemed fine. Do you have any idea what could have happened to her?

No, I don't have a clue. I'm sitting on the steps of the Faculty of Engineering and I don't know nor can imagine ever knowing in the rest of my life where Perla may be. I picture her dressed in immaculate white leaving her house to walk the twenty-five blocks to see Ema, Specialist in Beauty Masks (quite some title). Ema applies a mask, beautifies you, smoothes away the fatigue, the fear, the corruption, and sends you out ready to face the day. To understand why Motherpearl—eighty-five years old, husband long dead, skin like parchment, cranium disfigured by osteoporosis, ditto crumbling bones—walked twenty-five blocks every month for a beauty treatment you have to try to picture her hard at work in the tiny apartment that El Rubio (after years travelling around provincial towns looking for a job that didn't make him miserable) finally managed to rent so that the four of us could have a home; you have to picture her polishing the floors until they shone like mirrors, all the while dreaming of herself wrapped in big, fluffy towels, pampered by expert hands that would send her back into the world looking like a girl from the aristocracy, with her lovely face made even more lovely. What I'm trying to say is that Perla went every month for her beauty treatment simply because now she could and it mattered very little to her that her face was falling to pieces. Wrapped in those big fluffy towels doubtless she felt splendid and charmed, albeit belatedly. And she walked those twenty-five blocks to Ema's—as well as other routes to various destinations—because three years ago, sitting with Lucía opposite the doctor's desk as he had calmly predicted the gradual deterioration of her bones she, with the authority of someone who is always sure she's right, had said: Doctor, the day that I can no longer walk I would rather die. And she said it without a shade of self-pity because the years had made her wise. (Or perhaps she had always been wise and it was just that I, overwhelmed by her determination to protect me from every kind of misfortune, hadn't seen that at the time but only in the last few years when, drinking maté together in her house and cheerfully tucking into the croissants I had brought, I realised that, being so capricious actually made her a better listener, able to understand anything you might care to tell her.) So she started walking for the simple reason that movement is better than immobility and that if one has legs one should use them as well as possible, secretly knowing that if she ever stopped one day she would never start again. She used to look impeccable from head to foot, all in white, coordinating shoes and a matching bag and would set off on that day's journey like someone who has all the time in the world because old age had granted her enough serenity to sit down every so often in the window of a cafe to get her breath back and watch the world go by. And she always reached whatever objective she had set herself. Through sheer determination and sheer eccentricity. The only exception being that heavy March afternoon when she didn't arrive at her destination.

And there I was, sobbing on the steps of the Faculty of Engineering, with not the faintest inkling of where to look for her. I've lost my little rooster, taloo talay. The song came back into my mind and now I had time to ask myself where it came from. From Perla, of course, her song for lost things. It was infuriating. Lucía and El Rubio and I would be turning the house upside down in pursuit of the missing object while she hindered our efforts with her singing. For three nights I haven't slept, taloo talay, thinking of my little rooster taloo talay, I've lost it, taloo talay, poor thing taloo talay, last Sunday taloo talay. Where did she find them, for God's sake, all the pimps, the roosters, the blind girls, the handsome swineherd Jerinaldo, the shepherdess called Flor de Té, the poor old man who, from the tram, de dum de dum saw his daughter go by, a shameless hussy, half-drunk on champagne, there are just too many emotions, sometimes I prefer El Rubio, who has only one song. It's a very sad song and El Rubio says that when he goes to the South with his brother León, they're always singing it. It's strange to think of El Rubio and his brother León, who's quite ugly, driving along the road at night and singing something with the words little Virgin Mary in God's name I beg you, don't be mean to my papa, he gets drunk and often beats me, since we lost my dear mama. And the funny thing is that, the way El Rubio sings it, it's hard to tell if the song is making him laugh or cry. It seems to be a bit of both, that on one side he's making fun of it and on the other he feels enormous compassion for that unhappy girl. You can never tell with El Rubio. Perla gets annoyed with him because he sings badly and she wants her loved ones to do every-

thing well, but El Rubio sings whenever he feels like it. Calmly—
because he almost never loses his temper—but he always does
what he wants. He probably doesn't even realise that it upsets her.
The man's so absent-minded that every lunchtime when he leaves
to go back to work he says Bye lads. As if he had never noticed that
it's only Perla, Lucía and me around the table. Bye lads, just like
that, and it's even worse with the chandeliers.

The chandeliers arrive three years after we move in and
it's quite an occasion. This is the first time that Perla, El Rubio,
Lucía, and I have lived in our own house. In truth it's not a house,
it's a tiny apartment, and it isn't ours because we rent it, but after
twelve years of marriage, it's the first time that Perla has been able
to unpack the tablecloths that she embroidered for her trousseau
and a blue china tea service given to them as a wedding present. For a while the only furniture we have is the beds we sleep
in, a folding table, and a few benches. Every lunchtime for two
years Perla spreads out on the dining room floor the poncho that
El Rubio won in a country music competition, then brings the
table from the kitchen and opens it out over the poncho. When
we've finished eating, Perla folds the table and puts it back in the
kitchen, covering it with one of the embroidered tablecloths from
her trousseau. When it's prettified like that she can forget that it's
an ugly folding table and be pleased to look at it. As more pieces of
furniture start to arrive she surveys these, too, with quiet joy. They
are big pieces, polished to a shine and filling up all the empty
spaces. Only the chandeliers are missing. In every room there's
still a cable hanging from the ceiling and a bulb hanging at the

end of it like an affront. Until one day there's enough money and Perla goes to buy chandeliers. She tells us that they are splendid and for once it isn't a lie. One lunchtime I come back from school to find them in place. The one in the dining room is particularly sumptuous: ten lights above a shower of lead crystal teardrops. It hangs over the table and seems to fill the small dining room ceiling entirely. Underneath the glassware, Perla, Lucía and I sit ready for lunch, waiting for El Rubio, bursting with excitement.

His arrival is always a happy occasion. As soon as you hear whistling in the corridor you know that a few seconds later the key is going to turn in the lock and that before coming all the way in, he's going to peer around the door at us, as though checking that we're the right family. El Rubio has lovely, flecked eyes somewhere between grey, green and blue; beneath his wry, slightly sad gaze the world falls into precarious order. So, on the day of the chandeliers, the lock turns and he peers at us around the door as usual. The three of us are waiting expectantly as he must have noticed, because he doesn't come all the way in but studies us, disconcerted, from the doorway. We wait with bated breath. Finally Perla can't stand the tension and asks him: Haven't you noticed anything different? El Rubio is one of the kindest people I have ever known. He would never knowingly disappoint anyone. And so, still at the door, with that look he sometimes has of being all at sea, he struggles to identify the change that has us all enrapt. Finally his face lights up. With a complicit smile, happy to make us happy he says You bought bananas — right? That's El Rubio all over. So absent-minded and unassuming that he dies one summer without ever having told us he was ill.

Perla, on the other hand, hasn't an unassuming hair on her head. Not for her an unheralded death. It's more her style to disappear off the face of the earth en route to a beauty session. Sitting on the steps of the Engineering Faculty, I can't think where else to look for her. I keep singing I've lost my little rooster taloo talay and the worst thing is that I may not be singing it for Perla but for the lion. And for all the things that once were and will never be on the earth again. But especially for the distraught woman who doesn't know where to look for her elderly mother.

Grudgingly I got to my feet and went to look for a public telephone. There were no new messages at my house. I rang Lucía's house and listened to her voice on the Ansaphone but decided there was no point leaving her another message when I had no news to report. I rang my mother's house in hopes that the Guardian Angel had returned. The phone rang five times. Just as I was about to cut the line someone picked up. There were muffled noises, as though of someone struggling with the receiver. Then came the unmistakable voice of the chanteuse. She didn't say hello. Sounding bossy and a bit cross, like someone who has decided that, whoever is on the other end of the line must be the cause of her recent troubles, she asked,

'Who is this?'

'Mariana,' I said.

'Who?' she shouted. I forgot to mention that she was quite deaf so, as a precaution, I held the receiver away from my ear.

'Mariana,' I shouted, attracting glances from a few passers-by.

'Who?' she shouted again.

I sighed.

'Mariana, your daughter,' I yelled.

'Which daughter?' she said, as though she had a dozen. Then I knew for sure that, just as I had been fearing all afternoon, I had got my mother back.

■

That night Perla explains that at some point on the way to Ema's house she felt tired and hailed a taxi. That she gave the taxi driver her address but that when they arrived her house wasn't there and she didn't recognise the surroundings. That neither she nor the driver, who was very nice, knew how to resolve such a strange predicament so eventually the driver, poor man, drove off and she was left alone, looking for her house and not finding it. Then a very nice girl noticed her wandering around in a state of bewilderment. She asked Perla where she lived, called a taxi and gave the address to the driver. The driver, who was very nice, brought her home and there she was.

The following day she recounts the episode again. This time the inclusion of a new detail, in direct speech, reveals that Perla didn't in fact direct the first taxi driver to the intersection on the corner of which she lives but to another formed by the street where she lives now and the one of the little apartment where she used to sing tangos and where she closed her husband's eyes for the last time. I draw her attention to this, but she doesn't understand. Only when I'm explaining it for the fourth time does a glimmer of panic light in her face and she asks: How could this have happened to me? What's alarming isn't her difficulty in understanding something so simple; nor is that the two taxi rides couldn't have lasted more than half an hour altogether and she was gone for nearly seven. What's alarming is that Perla isn't the slightest bit concerned about this hole in her life. She seems not even to have fully registered it. How could this have happened to me? is all that she'll say every time she comes to the end of her story, and she's referring to the mistake made with the first taxi driver, not the seven missing hours. One afternoon, for the first time, she doesn't tell the story; just poses the question like an unresolved problem or a reminiscence. How could this have happened to me? We're in the living room in her flat; between us, the croissants that I brought and the maté I've just prepared, as though continuing with these rituals were a way to disguise some changes in the real world. How could this have happened to me? she asks out of the blue. This time I tell the story: her setting off on the walk, the tiredness, the first taxi, the mistake, the searching, the second taxi, the homecoming. Every so often I smuggle in a question. Perhaps if I catch her off-guard she'll end up remembering at which point she got lost, if she was frightened, if, like me, she sat down to cry on some steps. To no avail. Once I've embarked on the story, she seems to hear it merely as a kind of familiar music, an accompaniment to the maté and croissants. She only intervenes, now and then, to ask, How could this have happened to me? I've already told you a hundred times, Mother, I say eventually, because I'm sick and tired of going over the same ground. She doesn't acknowledge my exasperation. There is a long silence, then she asks again: How could this have happened to me? Then one day she stops asking; she seems to have completely forgotten the mix-up with the streets. The episode itself slips into oblivion. Along with the croissants. One afternoon, having realised that I can't stand watching her eat, I stop taking them; Perla eating is an intimate activity that only the Guardian Angel should have to witness, I decide. She never asks about the croissants. Nor about the maté. One day I stop making it for her but she doesn't seem to notice. Now, when I go to visit her, all I do is sit down opposite her and think of the lion. Its loss is an incontrovertible fact. I'm a suffocated woman with a decrepit mother. And my conversations with Lucía aren't about *The Divine Comedy* any more but about Perla's latest catastrophe.

I confess that Lucía and I were both too slow to accept that the repetitive woman we each visited twice a week and telephoned every day was not the same as the one who used to sing, in the style of a tango vals, the ten verses of *Nocturne for Rosario*. Perla always had a gift for persistence: if we were ever sad or unwell she, who considered such lapses a personal failing, would harp on so much about the neglectful habits that had brought us to such a state, constantly reminding us about her own infallible methods for restoring good health, that we ended up getting better just so we wouldn't have to listen to her any more. We were forever shouting at her to back off, because her overwhelming desire for our happiness was so trying, her love so selfish and prodigious that she turned into a kind of mother bear, determined to keep us away from all evil. She was insufferable, but a bit magical too. And we had taken it for granted that she would always be that way, so when her conversations gradually dwindled to the same few phrases, Lucía and I shouted desperately at her to stop, not to keep saying the same things over and over, that we had already understood, and we didn't even notice that one day Perla had stopped letting the Guardian Angel dress or groom her and that the person we sat opposite every time we went to visit was a dishevelled old lady with white hair, invariably wearing a nightie, who never asked about her grandchildren, didn't remember El Rubio and had absolutely no interest in how happy Lucía and I were.

It was the Guardian Angel who opened our eyes. One day she folded away her great wings and told us that she couldn't cope with Perla any more. Lucía and I looked at each other with terror. It was that terror that led us to the Happiness Care Home.

According to a second cousin Lucía providentially ran into during those anxious days, the Happiness Care Home was exactly the place we were looking for. All we had to do was ring a lady called Daisy to arrange an interview. She would take care of everything else. That was just what we needed: someone to shelter us in her bosom and take charge. I called Daisy. Her sunny voice promised the ideal environment to experience the last stage of life as a veritable paradise. Bring granny and her most important bits and bobs, she said, and while we sort out the details, she'll be looked after by staff who are so capable and kind that of her own accord she'll beg to stay.

So one March morning, less hot than that afternoon two years earlier when Perla and the lion were almost lost for good, Lucía sat at the wheel of her car and I came out of my mother's house on the arm of the shaky and demented old lady who had once been our Motherpearl.

With difficulty we settled her into the back seat. I got in next to Lucía.

'Where are you going?' asked Perla, as soon as the car started.

'We're going, mother,' said Lucía. 'The three of us are going.'

'What did you say?' Perla said.

'That all three of us are going,' said Lucía, shouting.

'Which three?' said Perla.

'You, Mariana and I,' shouted Lucía.

'I?' said Perla. 'I what?'

Lucía blew out hard.

'You're coming with us,' she shouted.

'You're coming with us?' said Perla.

'Not me,' shouted Lucía, absurdly. '*You're* coming with *us.*'

'and'

Under her breath Lucía said, 'You could speak a little bit too, no?'

'Isn't it a lovely day?' I shouted.

Perla seemed uninterested in my observation.

'I don't think she can see anything,' Lucía said.

'She can see a bit,' I said, 'but I don't think she's interested.'

'Where are you going?' Perla said.

'To a place I've been told is really lovely,' Lucía shouted.

'I doubt there's anything lovely about it,' I said.

'I didn't say it *was*, I said I've been *told*.'

That's Lucía. She can be ferocious all right, but she never, ever lies.

'Where are you going?' asked Perla.

Lucía murmured something I didn't hear.

'It's strange,' I said, 'with such dishonest parents, where did we both learn not to lie?'

'I taught you,' said Lucía.

'Ah yes,' I said. 'You taught me everything. If it weren't for you I'd be an ignorant brute.'

'Yes,' said Lucía. 'You *would* be an ignorant brute.'

Perhaps she was right. I've often thought as much. With such a capricious mother, such a vague father and given my own natural inclination to contemplate my navel, what would have become of me without an older sister to keep goading me onwards? I didn't say that to her, of course. I gave her a sideways glance: she was driving too cautiously. My worst trait is laziness, I thought, and Lucía's is wariness. And what about fear? Where did the fear come from?

'No speeding,' said Perla.

I glanced outside. To break the speed limit in these conditions would be nothing short of miraculous. We were advancing along Córdoba Avenue (if 'advancing' isn't putting too optimistic a gloss on things) at something slower than a crawl.

'I'm not speeding, Mother,' shouted Lucía, but gently.

I waited for an answer; Perla had never accepted that her opinions were not the only valid ones. But there was no retort from the back seat. I turned round to look at her. She was staring into nothing and seemed completely to have forgotten her earlier admonishment. She may even have forgotten that she was in a car with her two children. Or even that she had children.

'I think that it's the best option, at any rate,' I said.

Lucía looked relieved.

'Yes,' she said. 'Besides, if it's got everything they say, she's bound to love it.'

I didn't believe that she would love it. Rather I thought that it would be the best solution for us. She, all love and French piquet, had raised a couple of perfect incompetents who hated old age, feared illness, and were scared to death of this new circumstance flung up by fate (why hadn't Perla educated us for such an eventuality?). That was why we were driving, at walking pace, down Córdoba Avenue trying to convince each other that we were doing the right thing for our mother and for the world and that our destination really was a happiness home in which Perla would finally rediscover her gift for singing tango vals and El Rubio would peer around the door to watch her with his enigmatic blue gaze.

We didn't look back at her. Neither Lucía nor I looked back. We took it as a given (well I did, and I'd swear that Lucía did, too) that our mother was going contentedly towards the unknown. I didn't even think (I had to make an effort not to think it but I was managing that, out of a devotion to all that is beautiful and true) that to Perla, who had yearned to travel, this journey by car to the Happiness Care Home was probably much the same as looking at the sea, with El Rubio at her side, from the deck of the *Giulio Cesare* (something she had dreamt of doing so often, without ever managing a more glamorous crossing than the one across the river to Montevideo on the *Vapor de la Carrera*), or being taken in a coffin to the city of La Tablada, where he, affable, ironic and ever youthful, had been waiting for her for forty years—but not for this old biddy, please, bring me the one who used to sing tangos, says

El Rubio, from his sepia photo, the one in the little linen dress she embroidered herself in cross-stitch, the one who dreamt of being rich but who used to laugh until she cried as if laughing, when all is said and done, were the greatest fortune a person could have — and who could enjoy an anchovy sandwich as though it were a piece of heaven.

■

It was during that season, which lasted a whole summer and into the autumn, that the four of us lived crammed into a back room and El Rubio, for the first and only time, seemed settled. It was just after the time we spent living with our grandparents and before we moved to the flat with chandeliers. El Rubio had taken on the lease of a small shop and we slept at the back, me sharing a small bed with Lucía then Perla and El Rubio in the double bed, a yard away. It was wonderful: I could feel my sister's body next to mine and hear my parents' breathing, their hushed conversations. I didn't have nightmares in those days. It was a transition period, a time with no ties in which each person could hope for whatever he or she wanted: El Rubio that at last he would be able to buy the car he and Perla had been dreaming of, that he wouldn't have to count his pennies any more; Lucía that she was going to live in a real house where she could put together a library. I wasn't yet expecting anything very much — I wasn't even aware of being happy. (I learnt an awareness of happiness, I remember, one summer night four years later in the flat with the chandeliers. It must have been at the end of January because a few days later it would be my eighth birthday. We were going to have our first summer holiday and for the first time I was going to see the sea. That night I didn't need to hope desperately that Lucía would wake up and chase away my fears: she was as awake as I was and both of us were sitting on her bed, talking about the sea, about how each of us dreamt that the sea would be. At dawn we went outside to wait for El Rubio's friend to bring his car. I had never experienced the street at that time of day or the silence, heavy with people's hopes, that defines that hour. Lucía and I didn't argue about anything. Arms around each other, united in our excitement, we walked along the deserted street singing a bolero. That was the moment when I understood what happiness is.) During those back-room months I used to look forward to the hot nights, but I wouldn't have been able to explain exactly why. El Rubio used to pull down the shutters on the little shop, leaving the door open to let in the vibrant summer air and we would turn off the lights so that we couldn't be seen from the street and eat anchovy sandwiches made with pumpernickel and lots of butter and drink — beer for the parents, Bilz soda for the children — and chat, and laugh a lot, and nobody thought about death. And even though I couldn't yet put it into words, years later I knew that I had been happy.

There are moments in time when everything seems to be in harmony, I thought. Like the fairy bites.

'About time too. I thought you'd forgotten.'

And there was I thinking Lucía wouldn't need to interrupt me, now that she's a character with her own speaking part.

'I'm appearing as a character, but not to my best advantage. Let's agree that that car journey wasn't our finest hour.'

It wasn't the finest, or the most pleasant, but those two frightened women who were driving towards the Happiness Care Home were us too. That's why I have to talk about the trip. And why I've never been able to forget it.

'Speak about it all you want. But first of all tell the story of the fairy bites. I've already told you that I don't want to keep being the ogre in this story.'

I was just coming to that—the fairy bites. The fairy bite, strictly speaking, because singularity was part of the appeal: you didn't get more than one at a time. The fairy bite was an invention of Lucía's that came about while we were having our hot milk, and its appearance was independent of the shopkeeper game. I mean, even though we were playing Shopkeeper, at the moment in which she prepared the fairy bite, Lucía was Lucía. The fairy bite comprised all the most delicious things one can eat in the world, the golden crust of the bread, a lot of butter, the middle of the cheese, the best ham in the fridge, tomato, olives, if there were any olives, gherkins, if there were any gherkins. It contained everything necessary for an exquisite feast, but in such tiny quantities that you could eat one in a mouthful. It was like happiness: when you wanted to savour it, it had already passed.

Now we were driving a bit faster and in silence. There was a finality about the rhythm of the rolling car, something that smacked of death, but that was less august, more wretched than death. So I said to Lucía:

'Once we've left her there, we won't stay long, right?'

And Lucía said:

'Well first we have to make sure that she's comfortable and everything.'

I looked behind me. Perla was still gazing blankly out of the window. I tried a little experiment.

'Are you feeling all right, Mother?' I shouted to her.

She didn't even turn towards me but continued immobile and inexpressive, as if I hadn't said anything.

'Are you all right, Mother?' Lucía shouted.

'No speeding,' said Perla.

And that was all she said until we arrived at the Happiness Care Home.

It looked promising from the outside. White, two storeys, the front door and window frames painted green.

'It's pretty, isn't it?' said Lucía, determined to convince herself that everything was going well.

'It seems decent enough,' I said, not able to give Lucía full satisfaction, even though it would have benefited me, too.

Getting Perla out of the car was no easy task. But it wasn't the near impossibility of moving her that struck me; it was her complete lack of resistance to what Lucía and I were doing with her body. She's given in, I thought. She's finally given in. I remembered the lion and wanted to cry.

So there we were, the three of us facing that green door. On a sign to my left I read: The Happiness Care Home. Recreational Residence for the Elderly. I'm getting old, Mariúshkale, Perla had said to me less than three years earlier, and she didn't even believe it herself then. Now it had happened: she was incontestably old. All three of us women waiting at the door to the Happiness Care

Home were old. What kind of unappealing tableau would we form for the person who was going to open the door any second now? I could hear hurried steps from inside.

Now she stood before us. A robust lady in a pink coverall overflowing with kindness. They were expecting us, yes, yes, Señora Daisy was genuinely excited to meet us, and was this lovely lady our mother? I was too cowardly to look at Perla; I don't think Lucía looked at her either. We distanced ourselves, letting the lady in pink praise Perla and paw her, manhandling her into another coverall, this time in pale green. I'm not sure at what point we lost Perla: my attention was focussed on following Pink Coverall.

You could see that the place was well organised. Lovely chairs, lovely plants, lovely little old people with blank expressions dotted around. I tried not to look to either side of me. Walking beside Lucía I kept my eyes fixed on Pink Coverall, who never ceased doling out greetings and loving gestures, wiping a mouth here, rocking a chair there, spreading cheer wherever she went. She left us in a very tidy office and there, behind the desk, was Señora Daisy. She was blonde and buxom. And very talkative. I think she was already in full stream when we arrived, and was still talking when we left. It may well have been her natural state, as much a part of her as the big bosoms. Everything she said to us was wonderful. Even we, on her lips, were wonderful. She was very psychological and had realised straightaway that she was dealing with educated and intelligent people and that was particularly gratifying to her because it seemed that people on our intellectual level were better equipped than hoi polloi to appreciate the stimulating atmosphere of the home. From what I could gather of her speech, they got the old people to sew, to do embroidery, to gambol through meadows of wild flowers, and clap hands, and blow glass. I was trying to picture Perla—who had lately seemed so far away—physically cajoled into clapping games or sing-songs when, in the gap Señora Daisy left between two words, I heard Lucía shakily pipe up. 'The thing is, our mother is quite an unusual woman,' said my sister, incredibly, and I drew in my breath because now it had been said, and Señora Daisy was not going to be allowed to believe, like the police officer and monobrow and even the kind, dark-skinned girl that our mother was any old missing person. She sang 1920s tangos and said 'I'm stiffed' and wrapped herself in lemon-yellow feathers to look like an aristocrat. And she was so magical, that is her love was so excessive and magical that it had the power to chase away all misfortune. *Until the day I lost the lion,* I thought suddenly, and all the misery in the world came down on my head.

Without resistance (at least on my part, because by that point I had decided that it was pointless to resist), we were led here and there, chivvied along by Señora Daisy, who wanted to show us around the home personally so that we could appreciate with our eyes its delights, which were perfectly suited to a person as special as our mother. What rubbish, I wanted to say to Lucía, there's nothing special about Mother any more, or about any of us, all we have is the perfect memory of that beautiful thing we once were or of that which we now think was once beautiful. Balderdash, I heard someone say and stopped in my tracks. It felt like a dream, but couldn't have been because Lucía had clearly also heard it. She stopped and looked at me. Both of us knew there was only one person in the world we had ever heard use that word. Because Perla could lie like the best of them, but if she suspected the mere whiff of deceit in another person she would come out with those strange words the origin of which, even today, is still a mystery to me. Balderdash and poppycock. What's wrong, dears, asked Señora Daisy. We didn't get the chance to tell her: a small commotion nearby brought us all to a halt. Calm down Granny, we clearly heard a wheedling voice say. I'll give you Granny, said the voice of the chanteuse.

Disregarding Señora Daisy, Lucía and I rushed to the place from where the voice had come. We found Perla on her feet, holding onto a chair for balance and clutching in her free hand an object I couldn't identify but which she seemed prepared to hurl at the first Coverall who dared to touch her. Calm down, Granny, said the Coverall again. Perla raised her hand to her breast. Me, your grandmother? she said. And then a small miracle occurred: she laughed. And I swear she laughed with sarcirony.

Something must have come over Lucía and me because we pushed Señora Daisy—who was trying to hold us back—out of the way, then went one to each side of Perla. It's all right, Mother, we're going now, said Lucía. And Perla: It's clear that you two need to be kept on a tighter rein. We admitted that she was right and in the teeth of Señora Daisy's shrill explanations of how natural and even healthy our mother's reaction had been and how this little incident merely confirmed how stimulated our beloved and very special mother was going to feel in this optimal environment, we took Perla by the arms and made our way towards the exit.

We could scarcely contain ourselves, Lucía and I, we had to cover our mouths and stifle the odd snort so that Señora Daisy and the Coveralls didn't notice our predicament. As soon as we were outside with the door closed behind us, we exploded. We had to let go of Perla so as to double up and laugh properly, long and hard. They would have had her playing nursery games, said Lucía, weeping with laughter. And I said: That Daisy woman had no idea who she was up against. Clutching our stomachs we leaned on each other so as not to fall over, helpless with laughter beneath the recriminatory gaze of Perla who was gradually retreating into a world we didn't know but about which I, there in the street had begun to have an inkling. I remembered the *torrejas*. That afternoon on which we had such an overwhelming desire to eat *torrejas* that we couldn't wait another second before sinking our teeth into one. Then I, in the same way that I deduced every night the presence of the lion, worked out a formula that we worked on feverishly, perfecting it to a point where Lucía could have a go at making them. The end result looked more like dispirited doughnuts. It was wonderful, all the same. Pointing at the doughnuts we murmured *torrejas, torrejas,* and laughed so much that Perla, who was just coming home, heard us from the passage and when she came in and saw the doughnuts wanted to get angry but fell about laughing instead.

Now as then, I saw us from the perspective of Perla's empty gaze, laughing until we couldn't laugh any more in front of the green door of the Happiness Care Home. And there and then I was sure that I had never stopped knowing the lion. That, in the middle of the night I still conjured his menacing presence and, paralysed with fear and curiosity, I still waited for him to leap.

And I understood that the cruelty of life is precisely that: you never really lose yourself. Although the teeth may soften in your mouth and a mist of forgetfulness and tiredness cloud your understanding, you're still prey to the same vanity, the same fear, and the same uncontrollable desire to laugh that illuminated the other ages. Even if you have forgotten what you were frightened of, and there is no longer any reason to be vain, and you aren't sure what the hell it is that's making you laugh.

The three of us got into the car and set off home. Lucía and I not knowing what we were going to do with Perla, Perla not knowing where she was being driven, all three of us terrified and full of a sense of triumph that was entirely baseless. Absurd, devastated, invincible. Until the end.

THE NIGHT OF THE COMET

For Sylvia Iparraguire

All we knew about the comet was that someone had plunged to his death to dodge its arrival, that its tail had luminously sliced across certain nights of the Centenary Year of the Argentine Independence, that, like the Paris Exhibition or the Great War, its path through the world had memorably illuminated the dawn of this century. The man on the wicker chair had spoken of a photograph he had seen, he couldn't remember where, in which several gentlemen wearing boaters and ladies in plumed hats were staring as if bewitched at a dot in the sky, a dot that unfortunately (he said) did not appear in the photograph. I had recalled an illustration in my fifth-grade reader: a family paralysed by the vision of the comet passing through the skies. In the drawing the family members could be seen sitting at a table, stiffly erect, their eyes full of terror, not daring to turn their heads to the window for fear of seeing it again. (As soon as I said this, I had a feeling that the text referred to a Montgolfier hot-air balloon, but since I didn't know what a Montgolfier hot-air balloon was—I wasn't even sure that such a thing existed—and since I found it suggestive that I had attributed the family's surprise, whatever the real phenomenon might have been, to the arrival of the comet as early as the fifth grade, I didn't correct my conceivable mistake and everyone, myself included, was left with the impression that the comet was capable of sending people into shock, of leaving them frozen in their seats.)

We had a number of questions. How big did it seem when it was last seen? How big would it seem now? How long did it take to cross the sky? The man next to the table with the lamp suggested that, since it was as fast as a plane, unless one paid close attention the second it went by, snap, one would miss it. The man on the stool said no, that it rose over the river at nightfall and set over the western high-rises at dawn.

'That's impossible,' said the woman leaning against the French door, 'because then it would seem stationary in the sky. And something that seems stationary can't leave a trail on the sea or in the sky, anywhere.' Since this seemed illogical but plausible, several of us agreed with her. What we couldn't agree on was the size.

'The size of the moon,' said the woman in the light-coloured armchair.

'Of a very small star,' said the man who was putting on the tape of *Eine Kleine Nachtmusik,* and he added that it could only be distinguished from the star by its tail. And how long was the tail? The questions never stopped.

'My grandfather told us he'd seen it,' said the man smoking a pipe. 'He was in the courtyard, sitting on a three-legged stool' (I thought the stool was an aleatory detail and I immediately decided that his testimony was suspect) 'and the comet went by, neither very slow nor very fast, like a scarf made out of light. No: like a scarf made out of air that was also light, I think he said.' But, of course, this piece of information was simply too unreliable: given the age of the man with the pipe, his grandfather must have died long ago. Even if he hadn't made the story up (as the detail of the stool led one to suppose), who could swear that the grandson remembered the words exactly? And would he have been able to tell what was false from what was true? In fact, he had repeated the thing about the stool without lending the superfluous detail the slightest touch of irony.

But why were we to care what that grandfather saw? We had no need for grandfathers; our turn had come at last: it would cross the skies of our time. And we felt fortunate in those unfortunate days just being alive, still able to move around happily, still able to wait happily on the night of the comet.

Actually, that whole year had been the year of the comet, but since the previous week everyone's hopes had run wild. The newspapers predicted glorious events: this time it would pass closer to the Earth than at the beginning of the century; it would look mainly red; it would look mainly white but would be dragging an orange tail; it would have the apparent size of a small melon, the length of a common snake; it would cover seventy percent of the visible sky. This last possibility intrigued us the most.

'What do they mean, seventy percent of the sky?' asked the woman drinking coffee.

'But then almost the whole sky will be the comet,' said the man who had come with his girlfriend.

'Night will become day' (the woman lighting the cigarette).

'Better than day' (the man with the pillow on the floor) 'as if the moon, with all its reflected light, were barely a hundred metres from the Earth. Low down, in a corner, one sees the black

night sky, but all the rest is Moon. Can you imagine? Solid Moon.'
There was a silence, as if we were all trying to imagine a sky of
solid Moon.

'And how long will it stay like that?' (the man with his eyes
glued on the woman who came alone).

'The comet is constantly moving. It will move on and the
strip of darkness will become wider and wider until there's only
a thin thread, a thin thread of light on the horizon that will then
disappear and it will be night again.' I felt a sort of sadness; I had
only just realised that this thing which had once seemed out of my
reach—like the boiling oil thrown by the women of Buenos Aires
on the invading English troops in the mid-eighteenth century, or
the Firpo-Dempsey match—was not only about to take place; it
would also come to an end.

'But how fast will it disappear?' No one knew.

The woman with her back against one of the men's knees hit
herself on the forehead: 'Now that I think about it, no,' she said, 'it
can't be the width. The comet will take up seventy percent of the
length. Don't you see? The tail. It's the tail that will take up seventy percent. Like a rainbow going from here to there' (she drew a
vast segment of a circle with her extended arm) 'but ending before
it reaches the horizon.' She thought for a moment. 'At a distance
of thirty percent,' she added, with a touch of scientific rigor.

That wasn't bad, though I still preferred the vast Moon un-
folded a hundred metres from Earth. And at what speed would
that great arch of light cross the sky? That question—and many
others—remained unanswered.

But we didn't feel uneasy. Uneasy we had felt at the beginning of the week, when the papers announced that the comet was already over the world. We had always imagined that we'd rush out into the street to greet its arrival. 'Here it comes, here comes the comet!' But none of that happened. We looked up into the sky and saw nothing.

There were those with telescopes, of course. Those with telescopes made calculations and drew up schedules and strategic points. It seems that the brother-in-law of the woman caressing one of the men's ears, after consulting several manuals, had found the very best optical conditions: on the balcony of one of his cousins at 3:25 Wednesday morning with a telescope aimed at 40 degrees off the constellation of Centaurus.

'But your brother-in-law, did he actually see it?' we asked at the same time, as both the man and I played with the cat.

'He says he thinks he saw it,' was the cautious answer.

We had heard of some people who had travelled to Chascomus or to a place somewhere between San Miguel del Monte and Las Flores, or of others who had hurried to Tandil, to a small hill close to the Moving Rock. But as we had not had the chance to talk to any of them, we didn't know whether these peregrinations had been fruitful. Through adverts in the newspapers we knew that several kinds of charters had been organised, from a jet flight to San Martin de los Andes that included champagne dinner, diplomatic suite, sauna and full American breakfast, to bus tours to several suburban areas, a few with traditional barbecue and guitar music under the comet's light. We didn't know what the results had been. But three very precise lines in a Thursday paper made us dismiss all those telescopes and nocturnal ramblings. And that's how it had to be. Because what we had always dreamt of, what we truly wished for, was simply to look up and see it. And that, the three lines in the paper said, would become possible on Friday night once it was completely dark; then the comet would come closer to Earth than ever before. Then, and only then, might it be seen as those men in boaters and those women in hats had seen it, as the grandfather on his three-legged stool and the bewitched family in my reader had seen it. Right here, by the river, on the Costanera Sur. And, in honour of that unique moment for which we had longed since our days of reading adventure stories and which, with luck, would repeat itself for our children's grandchildren, this Friday night, all the lights of the Costanera would be switched off.

That was the reason that waiting in this house in San Telmo, among lamps and stools, was something of a vigil. Every so often someone would go out onto the balcony to see whether it was already dark.

'No use going earlier' (the woman drinking white wine). 'We wouldn't see anything in the light.'

And the man on the balcony: 'No, it's not because of the light, it's because it won't come over the horizon until it's dark. That's what the paper says.'

But at what time exactly? We didn't know that either. Darkness isn't something that falls over the world for an instant. True. But there comes a moment when, suddenly looking out at the street, one can say, 'It's night already.' This was said by the man eating peanuts, and we all went out onto the balcony to check.

On the way to the Costanera we said very little. We were crossing Azopardo when the man nearest to the sidewalk asked, 'You think it's appeared already?'

And the woman next to the wall said, 'Better if it has. Then when we get there we'll see it suddenly, over the river.'

'The river?'

I don't know who said that. It didn't matter much. I realised that I too, since I'd read the announcement in the paper, had imagined it like that: with its tail of powdered stars extending down into the river. But there's no real river in Buenos Aires any longer.

'Grass and mosquitoes, that's all there is on the Costanera Sur,' said the man on my right.

'Still the place has kept its own magic' (the woman behind). 'It's as if it has preserved a memory of the river.' I recalled the majestic ghost of the Municipal Balneario Beach, the square celebrating the triumphant arrival of the Solitary Seaman, Luis Viale, and his stone lifebelt about to dive (into a muddy lot where there are now only screeching magpies) to save the victims of the shipwrecked *Vapor de la Carrera*. I recalled the drawbridge, the same bridge I'd crossed in the No. 14 streetcar when my mother took me to the Balneario, so familiar that I could tell the width of the beach by the height of the water hitting the stone wall. I loved that bridge, the breathless wait on the days when it opened leisurely to allow a cargo ship to pass, the suspense as it closed again, since the slightest mistake in the position of the tracks (I suspected) would provoke a terrible derailment. And the joy when the streetcar emerged unscathed and the river lay waiting for me. The river was like life: the comet was something else. The comet was like one of those moments of ecstasy that can be found only in books. Distractedly, I knew that it would return one day, but I didn't expect it to. Because in the days when happiness consisted in playing in the mud of the Balneario, any comet or paradise glimpsed beyond my twentieth year didn't merit being dreamt about.

'And here I am walking across that bridge,' I said to myself, 'not so different from the person who once crossed it in a streetcar so as not to love it still, nor so decrepit as not to be on the verge of shouting with joy, as I march in procession to meet the comet with this bunch of lunatics.'

It took me a while to realise that the word 'procession' had occurred to me because of the mass of people who, on foot or in cars or trucks or even in a tractor, were gathering together in greater and greater numbers as we approached the Costanera.

The Costanera itself was a virtual wall. Between the crowd trying to find a good spot from which to view the sky, the smoke from the improvised bread-and-sausage vendors, and the absence of spotlights, the only thing visible from the Los Italianos Boulevard (where we now found ourselves) was a bloated amoeba of more or less human consistency, into which we were sucked and which didn't stop moving and humming.

'Over there, over there.' Not far from me, a forceful voice managed to emerge from the amoeba. Several of us turned to look. I detected a thin and knotted index finger pointing towards the northeast.

'Where? I can't see a thing.'

'There. Can't you see it? A fraction to the side of those two stars. About this far away from the horizon.'

'But is it rising?' asked an anguished voice to my left.

'Well, it's rising slowly.'

I thought I saw it, gently separating itself from the tiny light of a booth or something, close to the horizon, when behind me a hoarse voice shouted, 'No, it's there, far up. To the right of the Three Marys.'

I had no trouble finding the Three Marys and I was scrutinising their right side when I heard a child's voice full of enthusiasm: 'I see it! There it is! It's huge!'

I looked for the child's finger and, somewhat hopefully, for something huge in the direction his finger indicated. In vain.

'You know what the problem is?' said a voice almost in my ear. 'We're looking for it straight on. And that can't be done: it can't be seen straight on. What we should do is stand sideways and look for it out of the corner of our eyes.'

I turned halfway round. I noticed that several other people had done the same, only they turned sideways relative to different things. I shrugged and looked upward out of the corner of my eye, first with my right eye and then with my left. A hand touched my ankle. Startled I looked down. There were several people lying on the ground.

'Can I give you some advice?' came a voice next to my feet. 'Lie down on the grass. That way, face up, you can see the whole sky at once and I think you should be able to find it immediately.'

Obediently I lay down next to several strangers and again I looked upward. In the unlit and moonless night, under the continuous music of the universe, I felt on the point of discovering something that might have allowed me, perhaps, to continue with my life with a certain degree of peace. Then, a few metres away from my head, someone spoke: 'Don't you realise it's useless to look up from the ground? The trick is to make a reticule with your fingers. Didn't you read that this reticular effect increases the power of your vision? It's just like having a microscope.'

The microscope man seemed unreliable to me, so I never got around to trying the reticular effect. Somewhat disheartened, I stood up. I looked around me. Pubescent youngsters, hunchbacks, women about to give birth, people suffering from high blood pressure, idlers and matrons were simultaneously and noisily pointing at the zenith, at the horizon, at the fountain of Lola Mora, at the planes taking off from the Municipal Airport, at certain falling stars, at fireworks, at the Milky Way or at the unexpected phantom ship of *La Carrera*. Cross-eyed, frowning, using the reticular effect, twitching their ears, jumping on one leg, swinging their pelvises, using telescopes, microscopes, periscopes or kaleidoscopes, through engagement rings, straws, the eyes of needles, or water pipes, everyone was peering at the sky. Each person was searching, among the avalanche of stars (cold and beautiful since the awakening of the world, cold and beautiful when the last little glimmer from our planet is extinguished), each one was searching among those stars for a singular undefinable light. We never even realised that we were discovering death. And yet that is what it was: we had lost, once again, our last chance. One day, like a melon, like a snake, like a scarf of light, like everything round or with a tail or resplendent that we can create through our sheer desire to be happy, the golden-tailed comet would spin again through the space that had been our sky. But we, we who struggled and waited that night under the impassive stars, we on this bank and shoal would no longer disturb the soft evening mist to chase it.

Short-story writer, novelist and essayist Liliana Heker was born in Buenos Aires in 1943. She founded, with Abelardo Castillo, the literary magazines *El Escarabajo de Oro* (1961–1974) and *El Ornitorrinco* (1977–1986), where she published essays and sustained polemics that went beyond the issues that stirred them. Heker published five short-story collections and was twice awarded the Konex Prize, granted to the best short-story books of each decade. She is also the author of two novels, *Zona de clivaje* and *El fin de la historia*, and two nonfiction works, *Las hermanas de Shakespeare* and *Diálogos sobre la vida y la muerte*. Since 1978 she coordinates writing workshops, where she mentors many current Argentinian writers.

ALBERTO MANGUEL is an internationally acclaimed writer, translator, editor and critic. He is the author of numerous nonfiction books, including *The Dictionary of Imaginary Places* (coauthored with Gianni Guadalupi), *A History of Reading*, *Homer's* Iliad *and* Odyssey: *A Biography*, *The Library at Night*, *A Reader on Reading* and *Curiosity*. Manguel has also published novels in English (*News from a Foreign Country Came*) and Spanish (*El regreso* and *Todos los hombres son mentirosos*). Among his many awards are the Guggenheim Fellowship and an honorary doctorate from the University of Liège. Manguel is an Officier de l'Ordre des Arts et des Lettres.

MIRANDA FRANCE is the author of books on Spain and Argentina, as well as two novels. A regular contributor to books pages, she also teaches creative writing and has translated various works of Latin American fiction, including Alberto Manguel's *All Men Are Liars*.